VIVACITY

J.S.Court

VIVACITY

ISBN: 979-8-6285-8330-2

DEDICATION

For Leo
Autism Spectrum Disorder and Attention Deficit Hyperactivity
Disorder affect millions of children around the world and is one of
the most underrepresented groups in literacy and film today.
Accept
Understand
Teach
Include
Support
Motivate

CONTENTS

1	Just another day	1
2	Bootcamp	17
3	The new plan	27
4	Out of sight	39
5	Viva City	49
6	The baddest bad guy ever	63
7	King of the world	79

VIVACITY

VIVACITY

1 JUST ANOTHER DAY

It was always cloudy in the quiet village of Stormless and the rain had been falling all night. The day was just breaking and although the rain was slowing down, there were still a few drops gently falling on the rooftops. There were a few puddles along the pavement and the sound of water could be heard trickling into the drains. A tall chestnut tree at the fire station, hung over the front garden of number one Solitary Lane and its leaves were scattered across the grass gently blowing in the breeze.

In an instant, the silence was broken as the door to number one swung open, and a rainbow of color and energy seemed to spill out into the street from the house. It was Monday morning and Leo was just starting his short walk to school with his mother. He was wearing his favorite red top with his blue trousers and he carried a small blue bag on his back. His bright yellow hair shone like a beacon through the dullness of the morning.

"Slow down Leo," his mother called out. "I need to lock the door." He turned to face her. "I know mum, "anyway listen," he replied, speaking very quickly and excitedly.

"In Leo world," he said, "I'm going to have a great big castle and I'll make it from plastic bottles and cardboard, with four turrets and lots of flags that say 'King Leo' with a picture of me. It'll have huge gates at the front that turn into an evil face, and the bad guys will try to attack with their magical blue flames, but there's water all around the castle so they can't get in.

There are boats on the water shaped like Santa's sleigh, which the bad guys have stolen, and they're filled with presents for everyone in the world."

His mother put a reassuring hand on the top of his head and gently stroked his hair as they walked along. She often listened to Leo's fantastical stories and ideas with a sense of wonder and awe. "That sounds wonderful," she said, "but does there always have to be a bad guy in your stories? there should be a princess and a superhero, and everyone should be happy."

Leo pondered over this for a few seconds and then looked up at her. "You look like a princess mummy," he told her. Leo often paid her a compliment and calling her a princess gave her a warm feeling inside.

She had yellow hair just like him, but it was a little bit longer and she wore blue rimmed glasses. She had forgotten her coat and umbrella in the morning rush but was dressed for work.

Leo continued with his story just as enthusiastic as before. "I'll build a giant dolphin statue that'll come to life and swim up to the sleigh boats and steal the presents back, then I'll strap some ropes to the dolphin and ride it over the seas and the mountains, and I'll take the presents to all the people and......

"STOP," cried Leo's mother as she gripped him tightly by the arm. Leo was totally unaware that they had reached the crossing on the road, and he failed to notice the cars speeding past in front of him. "You really need to look before you cross Leo," she told him. Leo was always so focused on his imagination that he rarely looked when crossing the road and his mother always needed to be ready to stop him.

She took his hand and they crossed over to a wide alleyway, where some other parents were walking their children to school. Leo looked ahead and recognized a girl from the school walking along with her mother, so he decided to tell her all about his Leo world and ran to catch up with her. After chatting for a few seconds, the girls' mother looked down at Leo then spoke to her daughter. "Come along Susan, we're going to be late for school." She tugged on the girls' hand and Leo struggled to keep up. Leo's mother called after him. "Leo, walk with me," she said. Leo turned and waited for her, then continued with his story of adventure and heroism.

Before long, they had arrived at the gates of Lightless Primary School and as they approached the gates, a few of the other parents were standing in a small group talking to each other.

Some of them looked across at Leo and his mother, then turned their backs and huddled together more closely. They whispered to each other and gave an occasional glance in their direction, but Leo didn't notice. He was looking across at his teacher by the gate. Miss Orderly stood by the gates waiting for the last of the children to arrive. She was a thin lady with a wrinkly face and light grey hair that was tied in a bun at the back of her head.

She didn't speak to Leo or his mother as they walked through the gates, and the expression on her face was just as stern as it usually was.

The school itself consisted of several plain looking brick buildings which all had a flat roof.

The gates opened into a large playground with a few trees to one side, and there was a small pathway at the end of the playground which led to a larger sports field at the back of the school.

As Leo and his mother stepped into the playground there must have been at least 200 children running around. Some of them were playing Tag or hopscotch, and he could see a girl skipping by the old oak tree. All of the children were dressed in grey, just like the parents and teachers and he felt a little overwhelmed by all the commotion.

He could hear the skipping rope slapping against the playground floor and the sound of children chatting all around him in every direction. He looked up to see the trees swaying in the light breeze and there was a damp smell in the air. He could feel tiny raindrops on his face and his backpack was pulling on his shoulders. He closed his eyes for a moment to shut out the sound and then he felt his mother gently tapping him on the shoulder.

"Hey Leo," she said. He turned around to face her. "Have a good day ok." She gently pulled him to one side and whispered in his ear. "Please try not to shut Miss Orderly out today, you know she doesn't like it." Leo folded his arms. "But she's always telling me rules," he replied. "I know Leo, but please try." Leo smiled and gave her a kiss on the lips then hugged her tightly.

As he threw his arms around her and squeezed, his color seemed to radiate right through her. A warm glow could be seen in their faces and their hair started to change to a brighter shade of yellow.

Leo let her go, and the color returned to normal then he turned around and slowly walked into the playground. "I'll see you after school," she called, "go and find Misha."

Leo didn't look back, but his mother watched for a few moments, before walking back through the school gates to head for work.

Misha was Leo's best friend and they always met at the same corner of the playground each morning. She always wore pink clothes and had bright pink hair. She would sometimes flap her hands when she was excited and would often walk on tip toes.

She stood in the corner of the playground with Tom, another of Leo's friends, holding an assortment of cards in her hand.

"Misha, Tom," Leo called with excitement and he ran towards them. Misha gave him a hug and then held up a picture card with a happy face on it.

"Hi Leo," said Tom, then he turned to Misha. "You should just say hello," he suggested, "everyone else says hello, it's not that hard." Misha frowned at him and put her finger to her lips to tell him to hush.

Leo thought that Tom was the smartest person in the world, but he still often disagreed with him. "Why do you always say things like that Tom? You know Misha doesn't like to speak. Anyway, you're not perfect, you're always clumsy, you can't to catch a ball and you're always tripping over. You don't even swing your arms when you walk. None of us are perfect you know." Tom was about to reply but before he could answer, he noticed three other boys walking towards them.

Leo and Misha turned to look. "Oh, it's the Frank twins and Billy Blunt," said Tom. They were giggling to each other as they approached, and each of them reached into their pockets to take out a pair of sunglasses. They put them on, and Billy sneered at them. "Your colors are so bright that it's hurting our eyes, "why don't you go and stand in the shadows?" The twins giggled again. Misha put her cards in her pocket and tried to run towards him with a look of rage in her eyes, but Tom held her back.

The boys removed their sunglasses and then turned to walk away still giggling. "Oh, just ignore them Misha," said Leo. They're just bullies. Misha punched her fist into her hand, so Leo put his arm around her. "Come on, let's go and find Tizzy," he said. They looked around then Tom pointed in the direction of the old oak tree. "He's over there, in the shadows," he exclaimed. Misha grabbed Leo's hand and they all walked over to the old oak tree.

Tizzy was standing alone and looking up to the clouds. He hadn't noticed his friends walking towards him and seemed to be in a world of his own, so Misha tapped him on the shoulder.

He jumped and let out a scream when he noticed his friends standing in front of him. Tizzy had green hair and he wore green ear defenders.

He stood with his hands in his pockets anxiously blinking and sniffing. "Why didn't you come over to us Tizzy?" asked Tom. "There's too many people," replied Tizzy, "It's peaceful over here."

Tom scratched his head looking puzzled. "But you've got your ear defenders on, it's peaceful everywhere for you." Leo Interrupted. "Oh, he's happy here, aren't you?" Tizzy nodded, still blinking and sniffing repeatedly. Misha held up a picture of a love heart and showed it to him.

Tizzy smiled and then he looked across at Leo. "Please try to follow the rules today," he said, "Miss Orderly always gets so cross when you do your thing, and she said that next time she'll send you to Mr. Mundane for detention."

Leo frowned and folded his arms in defiance. "I can't help it if she doesn't like fun," he said, "there are so many fun things to do in class." Tom looked across at Leo. "You're supposed to learn reading and writing," he said. Misha held up another card with a picture of a clock, and just at that moment the school bell rang out across the playground.

There followed an eerie silence and a stillness all around which seemed to last for ages. Eventually, Miss Orderly called out. "Everyone to class." All the children picked up their bags and made their way into the building without speaking and the four friends reluctantly followed.

There were 30 children in Miss Orderly's class. The classroom was painted a pale grey color with a small selection of pictures on the walls. There was a row of brown cupboards to one side of the room where all the class equipment was stored, and the children's tables were neatly lined up in four rows.

Leo and his friends however, sat together on a large table at the back of the class, waiting for Miss Orderly to give her first instructions of the day. She stood behind her desk at the front of the class scanning the room. There was a large chalk board on the wall behind her, which seemed to be covered with an array of numbers and symbols.

"Today," bellowed Miss Orderly "I have placed a bowl of Broccoli on my desk. I want all of you to draw this for your art project, using the crayons from the cupboards." Her long bony finger pointed towards the cupboards to the side of the room.

All of the children quickly gathered some green and brown crayons, then returned with some paper to their desks and got to work. However, Leo had no love for broccoli, so he decided to slip across to another cupboard and grab some colored paints and brushes while Miss Orderly wasn't looking.

"You're going to get us into trouble again," whispered Tizzy. "Oh, don't worry," replied Leo, "I'll be really quiet." Tom joined in the conversation. "If you upset Miss Orderly Leo, our whole table will get in to trouble, and she would just love to have us out of her class and into detention."

Leo started to open the paint pots. "You never get in trouble Tom," he replied", You always finish your work." Misha held up a card to them both with a picture of a face that had a zip across the mouth. She then put her finger over her lips to tell them to hush. Tom rolled his eyes and shook his head, then he continued with his work.

After a short while, Tom and Misha had both produced a masterpiece of artwork. Their pictures were extremely intricate and looked as though they should be in an art gallery. However, Tizzy's picture seemed to resemble a pond full of cabbage soup. "It looks like a pond full of cabbage soup," said Tom. Misha started to chuckle.

While this was going on, Leo had finished his picture and had spent the last ten minutes building a tower out of his pencils. It was a magnificent structure, perfectly symmetrical and it had one of Leo's shoes balanced on the top.

"Hey guys, look at this," he said. Then he used his ruler as a saw, making the relevant noises and called out "Chop it down." He then hit the bottom of his tower scattering the pencils across his desk and onto the floor.

Miss Orderly was sat marking papers at her desk, when she heard the disruption at the back of the class. She looked up and called out with a stern voice. "I assume you have all finished." Everybody stopped what they were doing and looked across at their table. She stood and walked towards them, with her arms folded and her beady eyes looking straight at Leo.

As she approached, she noticed that Leo was covered from head to toe in several different colored paints. She stood in front of him, open mouthed with her face quickly turning a shade of red, and her eyes bulging. She then glanced down at Leo's painting. There was no bowl in his picture, but one large broccoli with a green stem, and the top part of the broccoli consisted of several different colored handprints.

"That's not what I asked for, Give me that picture." Miss orderly demanded while holding out her hand. "Weeesh," replied Leo "It's only a painting." Miss Orderly reached across to try to grab it. In an instant, a huge clear bubble appeared, completely surrounding Leo and knocking Miss Orderly off her feet.

Everyone gasped in shock. She stood up and brushed herself off with a look of rage in her eyes. Leo felt quite safe sitting inside, and when he looked up, he could see Miss Orderly furiously thumping on the wall of the bubble. "Put that force- field away right now!" she ordered. But Leo couldn't hear a word.

The bubble acted like a sound barrier to the world outside, so he just sat inside and smiled to himself. He picked up a paintbrush from his desk and he wrote his name in big yellow letters at the bottom of his picture.

Later that morning, Leo sat in front of Mr. Mundane in his office on a large wooden chair, with his mother beside him. Mr. mundane was the Head teacher of the School and was well known for his lack of enthusiasm. He was a very old man, with a long nose and several grey hairs protruding from his ears. He paced up and down in front of them with his arms behind his back and with no expression on his face at all, and then he stopped in front of his desk to look down at Leo.

"You have been told several times about shutting Miss Orderly out," he said, "but you seem determined to keep breaking the rules." Mr. Mundane glanced across at Leo's mother and continued, "I feel that I have no other choice but to speak to the school governors and recommend that Leo is removed from the school, he is simply causing too much disruption to the other children in class." She quickly replied. "There's no need to be hasty Mr. Mundane, I could take Leo along to the D.O.I this afternoon, and maybe they could offer some advice on how to help him."

While they were speaking, Leo had started to sing a little song to himself in the style of a rock song and was pretending to play the guitar. "I'm a star, a shooting star, oh yeah." She gently put her hand on his shoulder to stop him. "Maybe the D.O.I could give you some ideas on how to focus and listen a little better," she said.

Leo folded his arms in defiance. "But it's boring there," he replied, "can't I just go home and build my Leo castle out of cardboard boxes and glue?" Before she could reply, Leo continued eagerly, "I was thinking about my castle with the turrets and flags, and I think I want to have a picture of Misha on them instead of me, but it'll still say 'King Leo' on the flag's, and I can get the giant dolphin and…..

Leo's mother had to interrupt him. "We can talk about this later," she said, and then she turned to face Mr. Mundane.

"I'm sorry for all the trouble today Mr. Mundane, I'll take Leo to the D.O.I this afternoon and I promise things will get better." Mr. Mundane sat down and started to tap his fingers on his desk while he thought about her suggestion.

"Very well," he replied with a dull tone in his voice, "but Leo has run out of chances, I'll give you one month to change his behavior." She looked down and smiled at Leo, and then she took him by the hand, and led him out of the office.

Later that day it was raining as usual. Leo felt restless in the back seat of the car on the journey to Drab Town. He looked out of his window to watch the trees and houses rushing past, and he could feel every bump in the road as they drove along. He could feel the warm air on his feet from the car heater and could hear the squeaking of the wipers moving across the windscreen. His father was driving and was wearing his driving gloves with his leather jacket and his mother sat in the front passenger seat beside him.

His father glanced up at his mirror now and again to check that Leo was ok. They were talking about the events at school that morning, but Leo wasn't listening because all he could think about was how strong the smell was from the car air freshener. He pushed the button to his electric window to let in some fresh air, and then he continued to push the button repeatedly lowering and raising it. Every time it lowered; he opened his mouth to catch the raindrops.

"I wish the world could be a more colorful place for him," his mother said, "I know he shouldn't use his force field, but he just wanted to be creative today, people just don't understand him." Leo's father held her hand. "I know, but you understand how things are," he replied, "the teachers say that he needs to blend in, or people won't accept him, the world isn't ready for so much color."

She looked up into her mirror to see into the back of the car. "I don't want him to blend in," she said. "Neither do I," he replied. He turned his head to glance back at him. "Hey Leo, we're nearly there, can you try to sit still for just a little bit longer?" he asked, "I'm trying to concentrate on the road and you know that I get distracted when you play with the windows."

Leo stopped and looked up. "Daddy," he said, "when we go home, can you help me build my Leo world? I've collected lots of junk on the way home from school today, and we could build the castle and some buildings and trees, and then paint them so I can see what the real world will look like when I'm a real king." His father paused for a moment and then replied. "I'll have to see how much time I have when we get back Leo, we could be at the D.O.I for a while."

Leo sighed a big sigh and continued to press the button to his electric window.

Soon they arrived at their destination. Leo's father pulled into a space in the carpark, and Leo looked out of his window towards the building.

There was a large sign above the door to the building which read. The Department of Inactivity. It was a very old grey building with ivy covering the walls. Leo noticed a large symbol above the door. It was a white circle with a black 'X' across the center. The building was surrounded by overgrown prickle bushes, and ugly looking stone statues.

The place always seemed to be very quiet and empty whenever Leo was there, and he wasn't looking forward to this visit at all. His mother turned and looked back at him.

"Ok Leo, I know you don't like it here, but just try to stay calm and don't draw attention to yourself."

Leo sighed and nodded. "We aren't going to be here too long, are we?" he asked. "I hope not, just try to be patient." She said. The rain had stopped, so they all climbed out of the car and walked across the car park to the entrance of the building.

They stepped through the doors into a huge lobby, with a large brown patterned rug on the floor which stretched from one side of the room to the other. There were several portraits of very important looking people on the walls, and whenever Leo came to the D.O.I, he felt as though they were all looking down at him. The eyes seemed to follow him as he walked along so he tried not to look back up at them.

To the right of the room there were several grey sofas and to the left, a large reception desk with a well-dressed gentleman standing behind it reading a newspaper. A tall thin lady wearing an apron, walked in from another room pushing a trolley loaded with cleaning products. She stopped to lift a broom from the trolley and started to sweep the floor.

Leo's father turned to him with a reassuring smile. "Leo, you could wait on the sofa while we speak to the receptionist," he suggested. "OK daddy," he replied, "but don't take too long, I want you to help me build my Leo world when we get home." Leo walked to the sofa, then sat down watching the cleaning lady.

DEPARTMENT OF INACTIVITY

    Just in front of her, Leo noticed a large bulge under a corner of the rug and thought to himself that one day, someone's going to trip over that.

    He then saw the cleaning lady lift the corner, and the dust she had collected with her broom was swept under it. Leo was a little puzzled by this and sat scratching his head. "Excuse me," he said, why did you sweep that under the rug?" She stopped what she was doing and looked over at him. "We always sweep everything under the rug," she said, "it saves us a lot of work."

She then placed the broom back on her trolley and wheeled it through a door into another room. Leo looked around the room feeling a little bored, then he started to smile when he noticed how big and puffy the cushions were on the sofa.

On the other side of the room Leo's parents approached the reception desk. "We have an appointment at half past four with Miss Serene Bland," said Leo's father. The receptionist looked up from his newspaper and said nothing. He hit his hand on a small bell, and a door to the side of the reception desk opened almost immediately.

A small lady with thick glasses and short black hair was standing in the doorway. She looked directly at them and spoke sharply. "I'm Serene, come this way." They glanced at each other and then Leo's mother turned to him. "We'll be back in a minute ok," Leo gave them the thumbs up.

They walked into the room and sat on some wooden chairs, then Miss Bland sat at her desk in front of them. "I know why you're here," she said, "I spoke to Mr. Mundane this afternoon and he told me about Leo's behavior." Leo's mother smiled nervously. "Oh, that's great," she replied, and she glanced at Leo's father for reassurance and then continued.

"We were hoping that maybe you could arrange for a specialist to go into the school and sit with Leo to help him with his concentration." Leo's father quickly joined in to support her. "Yes, we've been asking about this for the last couple of years, but we've always been denied, we thought that maybe just a couple of days a week would be enough, and I think the school would notice a real difference if you could."

She looked at them both and shook her head with a look of disapproval. "A specialist in the school would simply cost too much money, and there aren't enough specialists to go around," she said, "you were offered to take

him to behavior classes on a Tuesday morning but you failed to attend, and when we called you there was no answer."

Leo's father quickly replied. "Yes, but we both work during the week, and the D.O.I doesn't offer weekend classes." Miss Bland slowly stretched her legs towards the floor under her desk and dug her heels in.

Mr. Mundane and I, have agreed that the only way to avoid Leo having to leave the school, would be to send him to Bootcamp.

It is here, in Drab Town" she said, "Leo will spend the next 3 weeks there, and when he returns to you, I guarantee he will be rehabilitated." Leo's parents looked worried and they turned to look behind them through the glass of her office window.

To their disbelief, they could see that Leo had removed every cushion from the sofa's and stacked them into a huge tower.

He had built an impressive structure with walls and a roof, perfectly balanced and symmetrical, and Leo was sat on the very top almost as high as the ceiling. He had just removed his shirt and was swinging it around his head, repeatedly shouting, "Look at me, I'm King of the whole world."

2 BOOTCAMP

A few days later, Leo and his parents arrived back in Drab Town. This time, it was for Leo's three week stay at Bootcamp. Leo's father pulled into a long gravel driveway, and the building looked much like the Department of Inactivity. Old and dark looking, with a black 'X' symbol above the door, but it also had another building attached which seemed to resemble a hotel. Leo looked out of the car window and noticed that a man and a lady were standing at the entrance to the building, waiting for their arrival.

They all stepped out of the car and started to make their way across the driveway to the entrance. Leo dragged a small suitcase along behind him and he looked back to see the track lines he made in the gravel with the tiny wheels. He could hear the gravel crunching under his feet, and he started to swing his case from side to side creating a pattern as he walked along. As they approached the building, the lady spoke first.

"Hello Leo, we have been expecting you," she said with a smile, "my name is Miss Dreary, and this is Mr. Grim." She wore a long green coat and looked a little tired with droopy eyes and short grey hair. Mr. Grim however, had no hair on his head at all, and he had dark rings around his eyes which Leo found quite scary. Mr. Grim looked up at Leo's parents. "Thank you for bringing Leo to us," he said, "we'll take care of him and in three weeks, you can return to collect him and I'm sure that you'll be pleased with the change in his behavior."

Miss Dreary put her hand on Leo's back to steer him towards the building. "Step inside Leo," she said, "I'll show you around."

He started to walk towards the door pulling his suitcase along behind him, when his father called out. "Hey, are you forgetting something?" His mother put her arms out in front of her. "Hug's first," she said. Leo dropped his suitcase and threw his arms around them both. The colors instantly grew brighter on all three of them, but Mr. Grim couldn't look, he simply turned away and started tapping his foot on the floor.

"Come on Leo, let's go," he said. Leo's face dropped as he turned and walked towards the entrance. His mother called out. "We love you; we'll see

You soon," but Leo didn't look back. His parents turned and walked back to the car. They felt very sad and wondered if they were doing the right thing. They held hands as they walked towards the car occasionally looking back. They climbed into the car and shut the doors, then slowly pulled away.

Once inside the building, Miss Dreary and Mr. Grim led Leo through a short hallway with grey walls, and quickly shuffled him through a door into a large waiting area. "Have a seat with the others, and we'll call you through shortly," said Miss Dreary and then she closed the door. The room was painted dark grey and there were no pictures on the walls but there were a few other children in the room sitting on tattered old brown chairs. Some were reading books, and some were just sitting quietly looking around. Leo looked up to the far corner of the room, and to his delight, he saw his friends waving at him. His face lit up.

"Tizzy, Misha, Tom," he called, and he ran towards them. "What are you guy's doing here?" he asked. "We were told by Mr. Mundane that we needed to come here," Tizzy replied. "Miss Orderly just wanted our table gone," added Tom, "I told you we would all get into trouble."

Misha looked at Leo with a beaming smile and held up two cards. One with a happy face and another with a love heart. "I love you guys," said Leo. "So, what's going to happen now?" asked tizzy. "I'm not sure," replied Leo. "but now that you guys are here, I think it's going to be fun."

After a while, the door to the waiting room opened, and Miss Dreary stepped inside with Mr. Grim. Following them into the room was another man, who looked a bit like a mad professor with wild hair and a long pointy beard.

Next to him was a tall strong looking lady with her hair tied back. She was wearing a pair of tight grey shorts, and she had a silver whistle on a lanyard around her neck.

"OK," called Miss Dreary, "it's time for your training. Don't worry about your belongings, someone will collect them." Mr. Grim stepped forward. "you will all be split into four groups with five in each group, and then a trainer will be allocated to you." Leo and the others were all stood together. "I hope they keep us in the same group," said Tizzy. "No," said Tom, "they'll make sure that we're separated," Tom was right. Each of them was allocated to a different trainer, and one by one they were marched out of the waiting room to separate areas of the building.

In Leo's group, he was the first to be tested. He was taken into a completely white room and sat in a white chair in front of a long white table.

Miss Dreary strapped his right hand to a small gadget on the arm of his chair. The gadget had wires that led to another white chair on the other side of the table. Miss Dreary placed a single snail on the table, then sat down. "First you must learn to concentrate," she said. "I want you to watch the snail and make sure that you don't take your eyes off it."

Leo looked down at the snail for a few moments and noticed that it had only left the tiniest trail. It seemed to be hardly moving at all, so he looked up to ask what this was all about. Suddenly he felt a sharp pain in his finger, and a loud buzzing sound echoed through the room. "OW," he shouted, are you kidding me?" She slammed her hand down on the table.

"Just focus on the snail," she snapped. Leo looked down at the snail again and it didn't seem to have moved at all, so he looked up. "How much longer will … OW," She pressed her buzzer again and simply pointed to the snail on the table. "Weeesh," he said as he looked back down.

Meanwhile, Tom was in a wide sports hall which had some climbing frames on the walls, and some sports equipment scattered around on the floor. The tall strong looking lady with the whistle stood in front of him with her hands on her hips.

"When I blow this whistle," she said, "I want you to start walking along the balance bar, and you have 10 seconds to get to the end without falling."

Tom nervously walked over to the balance bar and looked at it with a feeling of dread, because it was at least two feet high and very narrow.

The whistle blew without warning and made him jump, so he clambered onto the bar and slowly put one foot in front of the other with his arms stretched out either side of him. To his surprise, he managed to take three steps in a row, which is something he didn't expect so he smiled to himself contently. Suddenly, he heard a shout. "Catch." A ball hit him straight in the face, knocking off his glasses and causing him to stumble. He fell off the balance bar and landed on to his bottom with a thump. "Try it again," she shouted, "we haven't got all day."

At the same time, an anxious looking Tizzy was placed in a small room no bigger than a broom cupboard, with no windows and no lights. There was an old Television set on the floor in front of him, and Mr. Grim was standing at the entrance to the door holding Tizzy's ear defenders.

"You need to learn to face your fears," he muttered. "A couple of hours alone with these scary movies should help." Tizzy was shaking all over and he was sniffing and blinking continuously. He turned to look at the television as the screen flickered in front of him, then Mr. Grim smiled a cruel smile, and slowly closed the door.

Misha was sitting in a chair in the middle of a room with just a table and a tall spot lamp. She looked around with her arms folded, and she didn't look happy at all.

The mad professor stood in front of her next to the spot lamp and looked at her with wild eyes and a sly grin. He reached above his head and pulled a cord that was attached to the ceiling to switch off the main light but left the spot lamp pointing straight at her. He then snatched her cards from her pocket and placed them on the table in the corner of the room. "We have ways of making you talk." He said. Misha looked up at him with an angry face and folded her arms more tightly.

The first day was over and Leo was marched upstairs to the dormitory by Miss Dreary. She opened the door and shoved him through to where his friends were waiting, and then she closed the door behind him. The lights were switched off, but a full moon cast some light through the windows and Leo could see that there were several bunk beds around the room with some of the other children already sleeping. Tizzy stood with his hands covering his ears and physically shaking.

"We've got to get out of here," he said, "it's like a prison, these people are evil." Tom looked at Tizzy while wrapping some tape around his broken glasses. "You're right," he said, "we need to find a way out of this place, I think that three weeks is going to drive us crazy."

Misha sat on the floor and started to weep with her head in her hands, so Leo sat beside her and gave her a hug. "Don't worry Misha," he said, we'll get your cards back, and Tizzy's ear defenders."

Tom looked down at Leo "I saw Miss Dreary hang some keys on a hook in her office this morning, they must be the keys to the front door. I could see your cards as well Misha, and Tizzy's ear defenders. They were on her desk next to a pile of toys." he said. "But there's people patrolling the halls," replied Leo, "how are we going to get passed them?" Misha stopped weeping and dried her eyes on her sleeve. She stood up and looked at her friends with a smile, and then suddenly, she vanished into thin air with a soft, dull pop.

There was a short pause, and then Leo looked at the other two. "What just happened?" he said with a look of shock on his face. "Tizzy chuckled. "She can sometimes turn invisible," he said, "I've seen her do this before." Tom started to wave his arms around, searching for Misha. "Do you mean she's still here?" he asked. Tizzy shrugged his shoulders. "I'm not sure."

Leo was still in shock and he reached out to search for her as well. "How long have you known about this Tizzy?" he asked. "Oh, a little while," he said, "she does this from time to time and you can never tell where she is." They all heard the faint sound of a door creaking behind them and turned to see the door to the room slowly open, but there was no one to be seen. The door gently closed again.

"I'm sure she won't be long," said tizzy. Tom turned to the others. "Ok, we need to get into our beds in case someone comes in."

He turned to walk but Tizzy stepped in front of him. "Can I have the top bunk?" he asked. Tom tripped over Tizzy's foot and fell to the floor. "No problem Tizzy," he said as he picked himself up, "I feel safer at the bottom." They all climbed onto the beds and pulled the covers over themselves while they waited for Misha.

After a short while, Tom opened his eyes and looked up from his bunk and he noticed a pair of ear defenders and some keys floating in the air, right in front of him. He must have thought it was a ghost because he jumped suddenly, hitting his head on the boards under tizzy's bed, causing Tizzy to jump as well.

"Ouch," said tom. "Misha, is that you?" Leo said curiously. She appeared in front of them again with a soft, dull pop. She was holding a set of keys in one hand, Tizzy's ear defenders in the other, and her picture cards were safely back in her pocket. Leo was pleased to see his friend again. "You are awesome," he said. Misha passed the ear defenders to tizzy.

"What do we do now?" asked Leo. Tom stood from his bed, rubbing the top of his head. "We need to wait for a while until the hallways are clear, then we can quickly sneak out of the building to make our way home." Misha frowned and started to shuffle through her picture cards. She held one up that had a question mark, and another with a picture of a house. "That's a good point," said Tizzy, "How are we going to get home? It's a long way and none of us can drive a car."

Leo scratched his head for a moment in deep thought. "I Know," he said, "we can go into Drab Town and ask someone for help, they could phone our parents and tell them where we are." Tizzy adjusted his ear defenders and looked across at Leo. "We need to be careful of strangers," He said. Leo smiled back at him. "But all we need to do is just need to ask them for their name, and then they won't be strangers anymore."

Tizzy looked puzzled. "It doesn't really work like that." Tom rolled his eyes and shook his head. "Come on guys," he said. "Let's get some rest; we've got a long night ahead of us."

About an hour had passed and they had all fallen asleep, except for Leo who was peeking out of the door into the hallway. He turned to look back into the room. "Psssst, the coast is clear" he whispered, but the others didn't hear him.

"Guy's, he said, are you even listening?" Tizzy rolled over and covered his head with his blanket. Leo crept over to the beds and gripped Tom by the arm.

"Wake up," he said. Tom jumped with such freight, that he hit his head on the bottom of Tizzy's bed again, which in turn made Tizzy jump. Leo leaned over to Misha and gently tapped her on the shoulder. "The hallways are empty; we need to go," he said. She stretched out her arms and yawned and then they all climbed out of their beds to head over to the door.

They all looked through the gap in the door and could see that there was no one around. "Ok, let's go," said Tom. The four friends tiptoed quietly through the hallway passing several locked doors, and all was quiet except a faint tapping sound coming from Mr. Grim's office. He was sitting with his back to the door, typing at his computer.

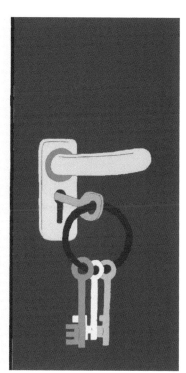

They all slipped past his office unnoticed and continued a little further along the hallway. They crept downstairs to another hallway and had to pass Miss Dreary's office. She was slumped across her chair snoring loudly with her arm hanging over the side clutching a bottle of drink. As they looked through the door, the bottle slipped from her hand. The sound of the bottle hitting the floor disturbed Miss dreary and she snorted and stirred for a moment. The four friends froze at the door and held their breath. Thankfully Miss dreary slumped back into her position and began snoring again. They continued through the building and finally reached the front door.

Misha carefully turned the key inside the lock and pulled the door open. She left the keys in the door and they all stepped outside gently closing the door to Bootcamp behind them.

3 THE NEW PLAN

The streets of Drab Town were dark and quiet at night. There were no streetlamps and most of the lights were switched off in the buildings, but there was some light from the moon which reflected in the puddles along the road. Just outside a shop window, Leo, Misha, Tom and Tizzy, stood together looking very nervous and trying to decide where to go. "Listen," said Leo. "Can you hear something?"

There was a faint sound of people talking in the distance, but Tizzy shook his head, "I can't hear anything at all," he replied. Tom rolled his eyes and then pointed towards the end of the street. "It sounds like it's coming from over there," he said. "Maybe we should take a look." They all agreed and followed the sound to the end of the street, then they turned a corner and in front of them stood an enormous white windmill.

The sails to the windmill were not turning, and it looked as though it hadn't been used for a long time. Attached to one side of the windmill was a two-story wooden building with a pitched roof, and there was a faint plume of smoke trailing up from the chimney. A few of the downstairs windows were lit up and they could see people moving around inside.

"It sounds like there's a lot of people in there," said Tizzy, so Misha held his hand.

Tom looked up at the sky, "It looks like it's going to rain soon," he said, "we should go inside and find some help."

Leo agreed, "I don't like it out here, there's too many shadows and dark alleyways and its freaking me out!" They all cautiously walked up to the front of the building.

There was a sign hanging above the door that squeaked as it swung in the breeze. "Run of the Mill Diner," Said tom. Misha smiled and grabbed a card with a picture of a Knife and fork, then started licking her lips. The sweet smell of freshly cooked food was coming through an open window and Leo's tummy started to grumble. "Oh, I hope they've got cake," said Leo, "I'm starving."

He eagerly pushed the door and they all stepped inside, but everybody in the room suddenly stopped what they were doing and turned to look at them.

There was an anxious silence for a few seconds, apart from the door that slowly creaked and closed behind them. Tizzy stood blinking and sniffing while still holding onto Misha's hand, then gradually the people in the room looked away and started talking to each other again. We need to get in and get out of here as quickly as possible," said Tom, "we have to find a telephone." They all looked around the room and it was a large but poorly lit area, scattered with worn out tables and chairs. They could see a lot of people eating and drinking, and there were several dark corners with shady looking people huddled together.

Just then, a bright blue flash of color caught Leo's eye at the other end of the room. He could see two people sitting at a table, wearing cloaks with hoods and one of them was waving a hand in the air to beckon them over. "Who are they?" asked Tizzy as he squeezed Misha's hand more tightly than ever. "I don't know," replied Leo, "but maybe they help us to get home." He started to make his way towards them, and his friends followed closely behind. As they approached, the larger of the two stood up and reached behind them to pull a curtain around the table, completely closing them off to the rest of the room, and then he removed the hood from his head.

He was very broad and tall, and a little older than the rest of them with wild red hair and equally wild red eyes. "My name's Bruce," he said, and this is Peppy." She pulled her hood from her head to look up at Leo, and as their eyes met neither of them could take their eyes off each other. Leo thought she was the most beautiful girl he had ever seen. She had long flowing bright blue hair and sparkling blue eyes.

As they gazed lovingly at each other, the whole world seemed to move in slow motion and Leo could feel his heart pounding in his chest.

Bruce distracted her by tapping her on the shoulder, and then he looked across at Leo and the others. "You shouldn't draw so much attention to yourselves around here, he said, where have you come from?"

Tom sat on a chair at the table. "We've just escaped from Bootcamp on the other side of town, and we're trying to find a way home, do you know where I can find a telephone?" he asked.

Leo Misha and Tizzy also sat down.

Peppy looked at Tom in surprise. "How on earth did you escape?" she said." Tom looked across the table at his friends. "It was Misha," he said, "she managed to find some keys and we all crept out after dark."

Bruce leaned over the table. "No one has ever escaped from Bootcamp before; we need people like you." They all looked puzzled. "Why are you both wearing hoods?" asked Tizzy. "We have to be careful," replied Peppy, "if people see who we are, we'll be taken to jail."

Leo was shocked. "Why would anyone want to do that," he asked. Bruce stood up and moved his cloak from his shoulders to reveal a logo on his shirt sleeve.

It was a picture of four different colored puzzle pieces joined together. "We're part of the rebellion," he said. Misha found a picture of a question mark and held it up with a confused look on her face. Bruce looked at the card, and then looked at Peppy. "Maybe you should explain to them," he said, "I'll go and get everyone something to drink and keep watch."

He stepped out through a gap in the curtain and closed it behind him. Peppy looked around the table at them all and took a deep breath.

"The ruler of the whole world lives a few miles north of here in Hum Drum City. His name is General Median, and he's the baddest bad guy ever. He hates color or noise and anyone that's lively or animated. He just wants everyone in the world to be the same. If people like us cause trouble, we risk getting captured by his guards, and taken to his headquarters for meltdown."

Tizzy started blinking rapidly and could feel his heart beating a little quicker. "What on earth is a meltdown?" he asked with a tremble in his voice. Peppy continued. "General Median has a machine on the top floor of his headquarters, and it's called the Auto Suppression Device or ASD for short. He keeps it well guarded and only a few people know of its existence. If you're sent for meltdown, the device will drain you of all your color, all your fun, and all of your imagination."

They all paused for a moment to think. Bruce reappeared from behind the curtain and placed some hot drinks on the table in front of them and then sat down. Tom looked at Peppy and Bruce while the others started to drink. "So how do you know about all of this?" he asked.

"Lord Pizzazz is the leader of our underground community," said Bruce, "he's the only person who has ever seen the Suppression Device and survived with his color still intact. He used to be a great adventurer and he tried to destroy it and free the color, but he was captured by the General's guards.

General Median was going to send him for meltdown, but he escaped by jumping out of a second-floor window. He was hurt, but his friends found him and took him back to Viva City.

Misha frowned. She held up another picture of a question mark and shrugged her shoulders. "This is very confusing," said Leo, "I've never heard of Viva City or Lord Pizzazz."

Peppy looked up at Leo and smiled. "That's because it's an underground community, it's well hidden," she said.

"When you mentioned causing trouble," said Tom, "what did you mean?" She turned to face him. "We use spray paint to write slogans on walls and

buildings so that we can spread the word about the ASD, but they get scrubbed off quickly by the General's guards, they seem to be everywhere," she said.

Leo turned to look at Tizzy. "What's a slogan?" he asked. "I think it's a type of animal," replied Tizzy, looking confused. "A slogan," Tom interrupted, "is a phrase or word that's used to advertise something." Bruce took the last few gulps of his drink and put his cup on the table. "Peppy is the best at slogans," he said, "she's super-fast."

Peppy continued. "Our people have tried to get into the Headquarters many times and Lord Pizzazz has told us that if we free the Suppression Device, the color would be released and everyone that's been melted down would get

their color back. The only problem is that there are dozens of guards outside the building and many of our people have been captured."

Just then, the curtain flicked across, and a tall lady stepped inside drawing the curtain behind her. She wore a cape with a hood just like the others, and when she removed it, she had long white hair with an Orange streak down one side. She placed a tray with cakes on the table and looked down at everyone sitting in the chairs. "We need to find Hope." she said. They all looked down at the cakes and eagerly grabbed one from the tray. "This is patience," said Peppy, "she works here in disguise and helps us to hide from the guards

Leo looked up to her with a mouthful of lemon cake and spoke with a muffled voice. "Well I'm always hopeful," he said, "I hoped for cake and look, we got cake."

Peppy looked at him with a solemn face. "Hope is her daughter's name," she explained, she was on a surveillance mission today at Hum Drum City but was captured by the General's guards." Patience pulled up a chair and sat next to Leo. "She's one of our best warriors," she added, "if we don't get to her soon, she'll be sent for meltdown for sure."

Leo swallowed his last piece of cake. "That's terrible," he said, "we need to go to the Headquarters and talk to General Median, we can tell him that he doesn't need to worry about the colors, and that everyone is meant to be different. I'll tell him that when I'm king, I'll switch off the Suppression Device and" ......

Leo paused for a moment with a sudden look of surprise on his face. "Oh, I need to pee," he said while hopping from one foot to the other. "The restrooms are at the other end of the Diner on the left," Patience explained, pulling the curtain across. Leo quickly shuffled past everyone and ran towards the restrooms.

"We must get word to Lord Pizzazz," said Patience, pulling the curtain back, "every hour that passes puts her in more danger." Peppy looked across the table at the others. "Maybe you guys could join us," she suggested, "we could use all the help we can get." Misha looked at Tom and shook her head, then held up a picture of a house. Tom looked at Tizzy. "I think Misha wants to go home, what do you think?" He asked. "Mr. Grim told me that I need to face my fears," he said, "maybe he was right." Tom thought for a moment tapping his fingers on the table. "We should ask Leo what he thinks when he gets back."

Meanwhile in the restrooms, Leo passed a tall mirror on his way out of the toilet cubicle. He stopped and took a few steps back to admire his own reflection. He stood in front of the mirror smiling to himself, showing all his teeth, then he frowned and made claws with his hands like an angry werewolf. He looked surprised as if he was scared, then he pulled a silly face while doing a little dance.

He then turned his back to the mirror and looked over his shoulder at himself while wiggling his butt in the air, then he made up a little song in his head. He started humming and then burst into song, "Lava, lava, lava, Volcano, volcano, I'm a superstar, I'm a super-star."

Suddenly the restroom door swung open, and a very large hairy man stood in front of him with a disapproving look on his face. Leo stopped what he was doing and hung his head down with his eyes looking up at him. He slipped past him and walked through the door back into the Diner.

He strolled over to where the others were sitting and pulled the curtain across. Misha immediately showed Leo the picture of the house, pointing at it with her finger. "Oh yeah I almost forgot, how are we going to get home?" he asked. "I think we should go to Viva City," said Tom, our parents still think we're at Bootcamp, so they won't worry about us and there might be a chance we could help to free the ASD."

Tizzy nodded in agreement. "If we could do this, there's a chance that people could get their color back and we wouldn't have to hide away anymore, things would change at school and we'd never have to go back to Bootcamp again."

Leo looked over at Misha. "What do you think?" He asked. Misha looked around at everyone, then looked up at Leo and reluctantly nodded. "OK, let's do it," he said. Peppy jumped up with excitement and threw her arms around him. "I promise you won't regret it," she told him. Misha looked at them both and folded her arms feeling a little jealous.

Patience stood up, "It's nearly midnight," she said, "I'll get you all a room for the night, and then we can head for Viva City first thing in the morning." They all stepped out from behind the curtain and followed Patience across the Diner, and then she led them through a door and upstairs to their rooms.

The next morning there was panic at Bootcamp. Mr. grim and Miss Dreary had discovered that the four friends were gone, so Miss Dreary anxiously ran to the telephone. "We need to tell General Median," she said, with her hands shaking, and she quickly dialed the number while Mr. Grim stood beside her.

At the other end, a black telephone sat on a very large wooden desk and started to ring. A smartly dressed man with grey hair and dark eyes picked up the receiver and held it to his ear. "Speak," he said. An anxious Miss Dreary spoke at the other end of the phone with a stutter. "Oh, hello General Median, I'm… I'm… I'm so sorry to disturb you sir, but erm, we seem to have had an incident at the B… B… B…"

The voice at the other end calmly interrupted her. Shhhhh, slow down Miss Dreary," came the response. She took a deep breath, and then continued. "We took in some new children yesterday for reconditioning, but some of them have escaped during the night, I think we need to contact their parents."

A furious General Median screamed down the phone. "Are you stupid? If word gets out, I'll have to shut you down you fool." Miss Dreary pulled the phone away as he screamed and even Mr. Grimm could hear every word. She slowly raised the receiver back to her ear, and there was a moment of silence before he spoke again with a calm voice.

"Try not to worry," he said, "I'll send out a search party, and when the children are found I'll return them to you in time for their parents to collect them, oh and by the way, if this ever happens again, you and Mr. Grimm will find yourselves in jail and quickly replaced with someone else."

General Median carefully put his phone down and turned away from his desk.

He was stood in a very large office with a huge rug on the floor. There were several tall windows along one side of the room with the curtain's half closed, and a few paintings hung on the walls. At one end of the room there were some double doors that were open, and they led to a long hallway. At the other end of the room, there was a smaller door that was closed.

General Median stepped away from the desk and made his way across the room to the small door. He opened the door and stepped inside then slowly closed the door behind him. In front of him sat a girl with orange hair tied in pigtails, and she was strapped to a metal chair with a strange looking hat on her head.

There were wires attached to the hat, which in turn attached to the chair and the chair had several wires which trailed along the floor to a short stone pillar. Floating just above the pillar, was a glowing ball of blue and green light which was slowly turning, and every now and then, there were tiny electrical sparks which could be seen jumping around the surface.

Just beyond this, there were two guards standing in the corner of the room next to a control panel which had several buttons and switches. "I finally have Hope," said General Median with a grin.

"Now, where were we?" he continued, "oh yes, you were going to tell me where your friends are, weren't you?" She looked straight at him with a determined expression. "I'll never betray my friends," she said, "my people are looking for me and we'll never stop until we free the ASD." General Median chuckled to himself. "Oh really," he replied.

He turned and walked towards the control panel. "Step aside," he said to his guards. They quickly moved out of his way and General Median looked at the control panel. There was an assortment of buttons and switches, a large lever to the right and a big red button in the middle. General Median rested his hand on the lever and turned to face Hope.

"This is your last chance," he said, "your father won't be able to rescue you this time." He paused for a moment then snapped at her. "Tell me where they are," Hope kept her lips tightly shut and turned her head away from him. "You've made your choice," he said. He gripped the lever and pulled it down sharply.

Immediately the glowing ball grew brighter and started making a humming noise with even more sparks bouncing off the surface. At the same time the lights in the room grew

dimmer, and there were sparks bouncing off the hat on her head. She closed her eyes and gritted her teeth, and she gripped the arms of the chair so tightly that her knuckles turned white. In a few short moments her bright orange hair started to change to a dull grey color and her skin became paler. It was all over in just a few seconds.

General median lifted the lever and he looked across at Hope as she slumped forward in the chair. The light from the ball grew a little dimmer again and the lights in the room became brighter. General Median looked over at his Guards.

"Take her away and put her back on the streets," he ordered. They quickly unbuckled her arms and removed the hat, and then they walked her out of the room closing the door behind them. General Median turned to look at the empty chair and the glowing ball of light. He smiled to himself and muttered under his breath. "Now come and get me Lord Pizzazz."

4 OUT OF SIGHT

It was early when the friends set off for Viva City. They were all disguised with cloaks and hoods to hide their color, and they tried to stay out of sight as much as they could. Leo and Peppy walked ahead talking to each other and giggling while the others followed closely behind.

For the first time in a long time, a break in the clouds revealed a glimmer of sunshine which could be seen rising above the buildings ahead. The ground was still wet from the rainfall the night before, but they could all feel the warm rays of the sun on their skin. Tizzy turned to look at Patience. "How long will it take to get to Viva City?" he asked. "Most of the day," she replied, we have to try to avoid the towns in case General Median's guards find us, so the route is a bit longer."

Tom was curious about their destination. "What's Viva City Like?" he asked. Bruce joined in the conversation. "It's underground," he said, "and its location is a closely guarded secret, Lord Pizzazz discovered the place several years ago, and started to bring people like us back with him to live there, everyone in Viva City has a job to do, and they all work as a team."

Just ahead of them Peppy stretched out her arms and looked up at the sky with a smile. "Isn't the sunshine wonderful?" she said, and then she took a deep breath to sniff the morning air then let out a satisfied sigh.

"It's never sunny where I live," said Leo, "it's always raining there." Peppy turned to look at him. "So, where do you all live?" She asked. "It's a place called Stormless village," he replied, "my parents didn't really want me to go to Bootcamp, but they said I'd have to leave the school If I didn't go". Peppy was curious. Do you like your school?" she asked. "Well, yes and no." he said, "everything's grey and the teachers are boring. The other kids think I'm too colorful, but at least I get to see my friends every day and break time can be fun."

Peppy gently gripped Leo by the hand. "Well you could come and live with me, erm, I mean us," she said, everyone loves colorful people at Viva City." Leo's eyes lit up and his mind immediately became a whirlwind of ideas."

Yes," he said, "and maybe when I'm king I could make Viva City really colorful and bright just like us, and then I could invite all my friends to live there, and we could have parties every day with balloons and cakes and ice creams."

Peppy looked puzzled. She was about to interrupt but she was suddenly distracted by a noise in the distance. "Someone's coming," she said. She let go of Leo's hand and quickly turned to look at the others. "There's a car coming, everybody hide."

Leo quickly jumped over a small fence outside a shop, and the others hid behind a parked car. They all looked across to where the noise was coming from, and a little further along the street, two black cars appeared and screeched to a halt outside a tall building.

Leo noticed that the wall of the building was sprayed with graffiti and as he looked closer, he could see the words, FREE THE ASD. Leo turned to ask Peppy if this was her slogan, but Peppy wasn't there.

He looked all around but couldn't see her, so he continued to look in the direction of the black cars. There were several men wearing military style clothing, and they stepped out of the cars holding buckets and brooms, then started to wash the graffiti from the wall. Leo glanced across to his friends hiding behind the parked car, and he could see Bruce pointing further along the road.

He turned his head and saw Peppy standing at the entrance to an alleyway at the end of the street, and she waved her hand to call them over.

"Quick," said Bruce, "let's go while the guards aren't looking." They all quickly scrambled to the end of the street to meet Peppy.

"How did you get all the way over here?" asked Leo. "I told you she was quick," said Bruce. "Come on guys, follow me," she said, "this alleyway leads out of Drab Town". They all quickly slipped into the alleyway unnoticed and soon, Drab Town was far behind them and the sun had started to disappear behind some clouds.

The group were walking together now, along a dusty road with a few trees along one side. They occasionally passed a house or a few abandoned factory buildings and they stopped every few miles to rest their feet or eat some food.

Peppy had been collecting some colorful stones along the way, and then she found an orange one and held it up to Leo.

"This is my favorite," she said as she passed it to him, "look at the markings all over it." He looked at the stone in deep concentration and as he looked, he could make out all kinds of wonderful pictures that seemed to be hidden in the patterns.

He could see faces and animals, and he focused on the stone for some time as they walked along. He eventually passed it back to Peppy and she took the stone and put it in her pocket.

As the group continued along the road, there seemed to be fewer and fewer trees or buildings around them, but in the distance a snow-capped mountain could be seen towering into the sky. "That's Shadow Mountain," Peppy told Leo," it's called Shadow Mountain because it casts a shadow over the whole of Hum Drum City." Leo looked up. "I'd love to climb to the top," he said excitedly. Peppy giggled at him. "It's the tallest mountain in the world," she said," and no one has ever climbed to the top."

Just a few paces behind them, Misha had noticed a butterfly landing on a yellow flower at the side of the road. She stopped and quietly tip toed over to Kneel in front of it. The others saw the butterfly and slowly walked over to crouch behind her. The butterfly had white wings with several different patches of color.

"Oh, it's so cute," said Leo. Misha carefully looked through her cards and held one up with a picture of a butterfly. She had a beaming smile on her face. "It's Beautiful," said Peppy. Misha slowly raised her finger and held it next to the flower, and then the butterfly climbed on and gently opened and closed its wings.

Misha carefully turned and stood in front of her friends to show them. They all looked for a few seconds but just at that moment, a faint rumble of thunder could be heard in the distance, and then the butterfly gracefully fluttered into the air while they watched.

Bruce looked curiously along the road towards the mountain. "Can you hear that sound?" he asked. "I heard it too," replied Tizzy, "I think it was just thunder." They all stood still, looking at the road ahead and listened for a moment. The sound continued to get louder. "That's not thunder," said Bruce. Misha held out her arms in front of her, mimicking the steering wheel of a car. "She's right, we need to get out of sight," said Tom. "But there's nowhere to hide," said Tizzy now panicking.

They all looked around, but all that was nearby was a big old tree with dark leaves. "Over there," said Bruce as he pointed to the tree. "But we can't all fit behind it," said Tom. Bruce quickly ran across the road to the tree and threw his arms around the trunk.

The others watched, and to their amazement the ground below Bruce's feet began to crack and the roots of the tree could be seen breaking through. The distant rumble of the car grew louder. "Hurry," called Peppy, we're going to get caught. His eyes and his hair began to glow red and he pulled at the trunk with all of his strength. With a loud crunch, the entire tree lifted out of the ground and then Bruce placed it on the roadside.

"Come on everybody, let's go," said Patience. They all ran across the road and leaped over the fallen tree just in time to hide. Within a few moments, a black car drove past them at speed, leaving a cloud of dust behind it.

They all popped their heads over the trunk of the tree to watch the car disappear into the distance, and they noticed a black cross on its door. "That was the General's Guards," said Patience. "Phew, said Tizzy with a sigh of relief, "that was close."

The dust settled and Tom looked over at Bruce. "That was impressive," he said. "I know," replied Bruce, "but I don't like to brag," and he lifted his arms to flex his muscles. "Come on," said Peppy, "let's get going before it rains." They all continued to walk along the road, now feeling more tired but the mountain seemed a little closer than before.

Tizzy suddenly looked up. "A girl," he said. They all turned and looked, and to their surprise there stood a girl with grey hair wearing an orange dress, looking up and down the road. "Hope," cried Patience and she ran to her daughter throwing her arms around her.

Hope just stood still looking dazed and confused. "Hello mummy," she said, "I can't remember the way home."

Patience looked into Hope's eyes and a tear rolled down her cheek. "Oh no, what has he done to you?" she said. She looked across at the others and could see that Bruce's eyes were red with rage. "We'll make him pay for this," he said.

Peppy held on to Leo's hand and a few drops of rain started to gently fall from the sky.

"Come on," Tom said to the others, "let's get to Viva City, it'll be dark soon." They all looked at one another, and then continued along the dusty road with hope.

The sun was setting in the distance, and it was starting to feel a little colder. They had finally reached the edge of the forest and just beyond the trees, they could see the mountain towering high into the clouds above. There was a small opening through the trees which revealed a narrow path leading into the darkness.

Peppy stopped and turned to face the group. "This is the path to Shadow Mountain, we need to walk just a bit further and we can get out of this rain," she said. "I'm not going in there," said Tizzy. Misha did a time out sign with her hands and shook her head. "It's ok," said Peppy, "we use this path all the time, besides Bruce can protect us, can't you?" He puffed out his chest and thumped it twice. "You're safe with me," he said, "I'll lead the way. Bruce stepped in front, and the rest of them followed closely behind.

They could hardly see the path in front of them and the ground was getting wet and slippery from the rain. Tom stumbled over some tree roots as he walked along, while Leo, Misha and Tizzy all held hands. As they tried to look around into the darkness, they could hear the rustling of bushes and the sound of an owl calling in the distance.

The walk through the forest was long, but eventually they arrived at a gap in the trees. Bruce stopped and turned to look back. We're here," he said. They looked across and saw a small cottage with a thatched roof. The windows were cracked and broken, and the paint was peeling from the door. There was a plume of smoke rising from the chimney and a faint warm light could be seen flickering from inside.

"Who lives here in this creepy old house?" asked Tom. "This is my Gran's house" replied Bruce, feeling a little offended, she's not expecting visitors, so I hope we don't frighten her." The forest was quiet around them and they cautiously followed Bruce to the door of the cottage.

He raised his arm to knock on the door, when suddenly there was a voice behind them. "Can I help you?"

They all jumped with fright, especially Tizzy who gave out a yelp and fell into Bruce. Behind them standing in the rain, was a very frail old woman wearing a cloak with a walking stick in one hand, and a torch in the other.

She removed the hood from her head to reveal her wild red hair, and she took a closer look at the group.

"Brucie?" she said with delight. "Hello Gran," he replied while he helped Tizzy to his feet. "Oh, my Brucie Woosie," she said as she hobbled over to him, "Give your old gran a kiss, you big softie." She gripped his cheeks with her fingers and gave him a big wet kiss, and then Bruce wiped it off looking a little embarrassed.

The old woman turned to look at the others. "These are our new friends," said Peppy, "they want to join the resistance and help us to free the Suppression Device." She looked across at them, and then noticed that Patience was standing with Hope holding her hand.

She walked over to Hope and put her arms around her, and then she looked up at Patience. "What happened?" she asked. She was captured by General Median," Patience replied.

The old woman turned to face the others. "Let's get out of the rain and I'll fix you all something to eat," she said. She stepped across to the cottage and opened the door and they all followed her inside, then Patience closed the door behind them.

They were stood in a cluttered room and could immediately feel the warmth from the fire. There were a couple of doors leading to other rooms and there were several little rugs on the floor. As they looked around, they could see all manner of odds and ends scattered over the chairs and tables, and some were piled almost as high as the ceiling. The furniture looked old and a little dusty, but the cottage was warm and inviting.

They sat on some chairs around the open fire at the back of the room, and Bruce's gran brought in a pot of hot broth from her kitchen. She poured it into some mugs and passed them around. The logs on the fire crackled with orange and yellow flames which reflected on their faces as they sipped on the hot broth. They all sat for a while and stared at the fire mesmerized by its warm and peaceful glow. Every now and then, the wood cracked and I tiny glow of ash could be seen rising into the chimney.

After a short while Bruce's gran broke the silence. "You'd better get going," she said, "we can't waste any more time."

Patience agreed. "We have to stop the General before he melts us all down," she said. The old woman reached up to a rope hanging from the ceiling by the fire and pulled it down. The entire fireplace slowly slid to one side to reveal a narrow dark tunnel which led into the mountain.

"Oh no," said Tizzy, "not more dark passageways." She passed a torch to Bruce and turned to Tizzy. "You're quite safe," she said, "It's time to meet Lord Pizzazz." They all stepped into the tunnel one after the other, and then the old woman slowly closed the tunnel entrance behind them.

5 VIVA CITY

The floor of the tunnel was wet, and they could hear the sound of water dripping as they walked through. The torch lit up the way ahead, but it was still quite dark, and Tizzy was frightened of dark places. He was breathing heavily and sniffing repeatedly, so Leo looked back and placed his hand on his shoulder. "I'm sure it's not much further," he said, "besides, we've got Bruce to protect us."

Misha was walking behind Tizzy, so she took his hand. Leo turned to look forward again and started to hum a little tune that he had created in his head, and then he noticed several brightly colored paintings of people and animals on the tunnel walls. "Did you guy's paint these pictures?" he asked. "No," replied Bruce, "I think they were painted by ancient people, but whoever painted them left this place a long time ago."

Leo paused for a moment. "It's not easy to see the pictures in the dark," he said. "I know," he continued, when I'm king I'll have lights put in the tunnel, and then we can paint more pictures. We could paint pictures of ourselves, and then we could have tracks on the floor so that we could ride a train to Viva City. We could take turns driving, and I'd have a horn to warn people we were coming…

Leo continued with his imaginative idea until Tom interrupted. "Hey guys, can you hear something?" Leo stopped talking and as they walked through the tunnel, they started to hear a faint sound of drums and music up ahead.

As they continued, the sound grew a little louder and then, Bruce turned to look at them all. "Welcome to Viva City," he said.

They all looked ahead to see a light at the end of the tunnel and Tizzy breathed a sigh of relief. "Oh, thank goodness for that," he said. They all continued to the end of the tunnel, and as they stepped into the light none of them could quite believe their eyes.

They all stood with their mouths open gazing at the view in front of them. "Oh, my O-M-G," said Leo, as he looked around.

They all looked across at a vast cave hundreds of feet high and stretching at least a mile in every direction.

There were trees scattered all around which had leaves of all different Shades of yellow, red and orange. Some of them were a hundred feet tall and some had treehouses built into the branches. There were people splashing around in a nearby pool and others swinging from ropes that were tied to the trees. Music and laughter could be heard all around them.

They noticed that the cave walls were covered in a myriad of colored jewels of all different shapes and sizes, which seemed to cast a light across the entire city. There were beautiful colored birds soaring above their heads, and a cluster of butterflies could be seen fluttering over the surrounding flowers.

Peppy spoke first. "This is our home," she said, we've got everything we need. We grow our own food and sell it in the shops, and we have our own currency to buy it. There's a school and a hospital with doctors and nurses, and Lord Pizzazz rules the city from his Temple.

"It's so colorful," said Tom, "How on earth have you kept this place a secret?" Patience turned to face the group while holding on to Hope's hand. "All of you are part of our secret now," she said. I'm going to take Hope to see Lord Pizzazz and I need someone to fetch the Dr?" Bruce nodded and turned to walk away. "I'll go with you," said Tom, so Bruce led him along a path through some trees.

Patience then turned to Peppy. "You can show our new friends around," she said, "and then I need you to come and meet us at the temple so that we can figure out how to stop General Median." She looked down at Hope and they both started to walk along a stone path towards the temple.

The others watched as they walked away then Peppy turned to speak. "Shall we go and explore"? she said with a beaming smile. Leo jumped up and down with excitement. "Come on guys," he said to Tizzy and Misha, "this is going to be awesome." Misha grabbed some cards from her pocket and shuffled through them, and then she held up a picture of a smiling face, a thumb's up and a picture of a butterfly.

Tizzy smiled too but looked a little overwhelmed by all the color and the noise.

They started walking deeper into the cave, and as they looked around, they could see rabbits and squirrels hopping about on the grass. "Hello Peppy," a voice called. A tall lady with a blue and pink stripped dress approached them holding a baby in her arms, and she was followed by three small children.

"Who are your friends?" she asked. "Hello Melody," replied Peppy, "this is Leo, Misha and Tizzy, they want to join us and help us to fight the General." Melody looked at them while gently rocking the baby. "Well, you are all very welcome," she said with a smile. The other children were curious of the new arrivals but a little shy, so they stood behind Melody peeking at them.

Tizzy continued to look around at everything nervously twitching and started to squeeze Misha's hand. Misha tapped Leo on the shoulder and pointed at Tizzy. "It's too much for him," said Leo, "we need to find a quiet place." Melody turned to Peppy. "You could take him to Zone 3," she suggested. "What's Zone 3," asked Tizzy as he looked up to her. "It's a bit quieter than here," she replied. "It's a good idea," said Peppy, "I'll show you the way."

They all said goodbye to Melody, then Peppy led them down a different path. They walked through some trees and the noise behind them began to fade. They continued across a wooden bridge which crossed over a stream and eventually, the path opened into a clearing.

In front of them was a small pond surrounded by flowers and bushes, with a family of ducks swimming on the surface. As they paddled, they left a series of ripples on the water and there was a colorful reflection from the jewels on the cave walls.

Misha noticed that there was a small bench by the side of the pond, so she took Tizzy by the hand and they all walked over to the bench to sit down. It felt very calm by the pond, so Misha reached over to Tizzy and gently lifted his ear defenders from his head. He panicked a little at first, but then he realized just how peaceful it was. Misha smiled and took his hand again, then he completely stopped twitching and leaned back sniffing the air, with his eyes shut.

They all sat for a few moments listening to the trickling of the water and the birds singing above, then Peppy looked at Leo. "Do you want to see something wonderful?" she asked.

Leo looked over at Misha and Tizzy, and then Misha nodded and looked back at the pond. "We'll stay here for a while," said Tizzy, so Leo and Peppy left them in peace on the bench.

On the other side of the cave stood an ancient stone temple, with high walls covered with ivy, and there were large steps leading up to the main entrance. Some of the columns and archways were broken, but the building was still impressive.

Red and blue glass could be seen in all the windows and the walls were carved with all kinds of shapes and symbols.

Tom and Bruce had found the doctor and they were making their way to the temple. The doctor hurried along behind them wearing a long white coat and he carried a small bag in his hand. They all climbed the steps to the entrance and walked through the main doors. In front of them was a long hallway with red carpets and there were several doors leading into different rooms. At the end of the hallway was a set of large double doors.

"That's the throne room," said Bruce as he led them along the hallway to the door, then he pushed it open and they all walked through. The red carpet from the hallway continued into the throne room. It was a long room with high ceilings, and at least a dozen stone Columns were lined up through the center leading up to a huge golden throne covered in jewels. There was another smaller chair next to this which was just as impressive, and surrounding the walls were several sculptures of animals, and paintings that were hanging between the colored glass windows.

They could see Patience and Hope standing beside a man in a wheelchair. He turned to look at them and waved his hand in the air. "Come in, come in," he called. They all hurried across towards the throne and as they approached, Tom got his first look at the leader of Viva City.

He was a very colorful man with wild eyes and spiked hair which had at least 6 colors, and he wore thick rimmed blue glasses and had a golden cape thrown over his shoulders. He looked up at the doctor while leaning over to hold on to Hope's hand.

"Is there anything you can do for her?" he asked. "All I can do is try," replied the doctor, then he knelt down in front of her, and gently placed his hand on her forehead.

He closed his eyes and started to concentrate, then after a few seconds a warm glow could be seen coming from his hand and his dark blue hair started to glow a little brighter.

As they all looked at Hope, some of the orange started to return to her hair and her skin began to look less pale. A few moments passed and the doctor pulled his hand away, then slumped to the floor beside her.

His hair darkened again, and he looked exhausted.

Bruce and Tom ran over to help him, and Patience turned to hope. "How do you feel?" she asked. Hope blinked a few times, and then looked up to her. "I'm ok, just a little tired," she replied. "Do you remember what happened to you?" Hope paused to think for a moment. "I think so," she said, "Yes, I found a hidden doorway at the back of the Headquarters, but the General's guards were waiting for me." They led me through the building, and then strapped me to a chair in the room where they keep the Suppression Device. It was so beautiful," she said, and then she paused to think about it. Tom looked up, "What happened then?" he asked. "After that, General Median pulled a switch and that's all I can remember", she said. There was a moment of silence in the room, and then Lord Pizzazz spun his wheelchair to face Tom and Bruce.

"We need the others," he said, "find Peppy and your new friends, then we can try to think of a plan." He looked back at Patience and Hope. "She has some of her color, but the only way to get it all back is to find a way into the Headquarters. Hope and the doctor need to stay here to rest for a while, but the rest of us have lots of work to do." Bruce nodded, "We'll be back soon," he said. They turned and left the throne room to find the others.

Meanwhile, Leo and Peppy could be seen hurrying along the path to the far side of the cave. Peppy pulled on Leo's hand as they skipped past the colored flowers and trees, then she stopped as they reached a small wooden bridge that crossed over the stream.

"Look Leo," she said as she pointed to the top of the cave. "Aren't they beautiful?" Leo looked up and he could see dozens of brightly colored parrots flying in groups, souring and diving in all directions. "They only live here in the cave," she added, "they can't be found anywhere else in the world." She looked at Leo for a moment as he stood watching the birds, and then she tugged on his hand. "Come on, we're nearly there."

As they crossed over the bridge, Leo looked over to one side where he could see a small cave entrance in the far wall. "What's over there?" he asked. "Those are the echo tunnels," she replied, "we can go there later, but first I want to show you the falls." They brushed past some flowers, disturbing a group of butterflies which fluttered around their heads before rising above the trees.

They skipped along the edge of the stream, and Leo could hear the sound of rushing water growing louder up ahead. Soon the path came to an end by some trees. "We're here," said Peppy. She pulled a branch from a tree to one side and revealed a cluster of small waterfalls at the back of the cave.

The water appeared to pour through some cracks in the wall above and glistened in the light from the precious gems. It cascaded onto the rocks below creating a small pool which led into the stream, and there were a few steppingstones leading into the largest of the falls. Leo turned to Peppy.

"Where does the water come from?" he asked. "The top of the mountain is covered in snow," she replied. "It filters through the rocks until it finally reaches here. It's pure enough to drink, and it feeds all the plants in Viva City. We can cross the stones and stand under the falls if you want," she said. "But we'll get wet," he replied. She smiled at Leo and stepped onto the stones. Leo reluctantly followed her across and watched her as she disappeared under the water.

As Leo stepped into the falls, he started to shiver. "It's really cold," he said, "quick, hold my hands." She reached over to him and as their hands touched; his protective bubble appeared and surrounded them both. The water hit the top of the bubble and trickled down the sides. "That's better," he said. "Oh wow," said Peppy in amazement, "how do you do that?" Leo shrugged his shoulders. "I don't know, I've always been able to do it."

They gazed into each other's eyes for a moment with their hair still dripping with water, then peppy spoke. "If you build a castle Leo, can I come and live there with you?" she asked. He nodded. "Of course, but you would have to marry me so that you could be the queen." They paused for a moment, and then slowly leaned towards each other with pursed lips. They were about to kiss, but peppy noticed movement out of the corner of her eye and turned to look over the pool.

"It's your friends," she said. Leo turned to look. "Are you kidding me?" he said. He stamped his foot on the floor and his bubble burst immediately, letting the cold water fall once again on to their heads. "Come on Leo," she said, "let's see what they want." They carefully stepped back over the wet stones to greet their friends.

What are you doing behind the water?" asked Tom. "Nothing," replied Leo. Peppy, looked a little embarrassed. "We were just talking," she said. Misha stood beside Tizzy with her arms folded and a suspicious look in her eyes.

Tizzy stepped forward. He was wearing his ear defenders again, but he looked a lot calmer than usual. "Lord Pizzazz wants to meet all of us at his temple," he said. "Can we get something to eat first?" asked Leo.

"I'm pretty sure we can get some food at the temple," replied Bruce, "Come on, let's get going." Bruce led the way and they all set off along the path.

Back at the temple the doctor had recovered and was stood in front of Lord Pizzazz holding his wheelchair. Lord Pizzazz was now sat on his golden throne and Patience was stood beside him. The doctor pushed the wheelchair and placed it to one side.

"We need to make a deal with the General," he suggested, "otherwise my wife could be melted down." Patience sat down beside Lord Pizzazz on the smaller chair. "General Median is not a man of his word, he would deceive you and throw you in jail with her," she said. "So how am I supposed to get her back?" he snapped. Lord Pizzazz leaned forward." We will find a way but we're getting too old for this now, the younger ones are our future and we need their help to change this world."

Just then the door behind them creaked, and Lord Pizzazz looked up to see Bruce walk through with the others following behind. Leo stopped and scanned the room with his mouth wide open. "Is this for real?" he said. He gazed in amazement at the sculptures and the colorful paintings on the walls. He wasn't worried about these paintings looking down at him, unlike the portraits at the D.O.I, because these were paintings of color and patterns instead of portraits of old people.

Lord Pizzazz waved his arms in the air and called out across the room. His tone had completely changed, and he now sounded positively excitable. "Hello, it's wonderful to see you all," he said, and he started to laugh, "Come, come, come, we need to talk." They all made their way across the room to stand in front of him and he looked at Peppy.

"Did you complete your mission?" he asked. "Yes, "she said, I sprayed at least fifty slogans on the buildings around Drab Town last night, but the General's guards were everywhere, and they were all scrubbed off again by the morning."

Lord Pizzazz frowned and thumped his hand on the arm of his throne. He paused for a moment, and then looked up at them with a smile on his face again. "Oh well, we can find another way to spread the word," he said.

"Is it true that you've seen the Suppression Device asked Leo?" Lord Pizzazz lowered his head in deep thought. "Yes, it's true," he said, and then he looked up again, "sit down and I'll tell you my story." They all sat on the floor in front of him eagerly waiting for his tale of adventure.

"It all started many years ago when I was a young man and still had use of my legs. General Tom Medial was a promising young soldier in the Great War, and because of his bravery he moved quickly through the ranks, eventually becoming Commander of a huge army. All the while, his beautiful and colorful fiancée was at his side to support him and they were very much in love. He called her the love of his life and he told her that one day, they would be rich and get married.

During his command he appointed the world's cleverest scientist to create a device that could cure the world of disease. The device was a success and many people were saved, but the war finally came to an end and as time went on, he became greedy for more money and fame. He started to work in the city as the boss of a security firm, but he lost sight of what was important and before long General Median and his beautiful fiancée drifted apart.

She left him but found love again with a young adventurer, and they travelled the world together. They had a daughter and eventually they settled down to live in Hum Drum City.

Meanwhile the General had become the prime master and had control of everything. He had grown to hate color and he ordered his scientist to alter the device, so that it could take the color from anyone that refused to follow his rules. At the same time, he had also discovered that the love of his life was now living in Hum Drum City with her new family, and he became enraged with jealousy.

He kidnapped her, and when she refused to go back to him, he strapped her to the meltdown chair. Just as he pulled the lever to the device, her new husband burst into the room and stopped him, but not before it had taken some of the color from her."

Lord Pizzazz was looking down at the floor of the throne room and clenching his fists in anger, so Patience put her hand on his shoulder. Tom looked at them both. "You were the adventurers in the story," he said. The rest of the group were totally mesmerized by the tale of loss and heroism but none more so than Leo.

I bet he feels really bad about what he's done," he said, "we should bring him here and show him how happy we all are and maybe we could get him to switch off the Device himself." Bruce didn't like this idea at all. "We could never bring him here," he said, "have you forgotten what he did to hope? He would do the same to the rest of us." Patience agreed. "The General cannot see the world the way that we do, and he doesn't feel there's a place for people like us," she said.

"Well then, we should go to him at his Headquarters," replied Leo, "then we could show him how good we are at doing things without following his rules, "we could show him how creative we all are, and that Tom is super clever and Misha can disappear."

Lord Pizzazz leaned forward. "It sounds like the right thing to do," he said, "but the General is always trying to stop us from spreading the word, and he simply wouldn't listen to you." Leo stamped his foot on the floor. "Why does no one ever listen to me?" he said. "We listen to you all the time," replied Tom, "you never stop talking."

Leo growled and clenched his fists out of frustration. "Well I'm going to see General median tomorrow, and I'm going to tell him that people like us don't need to be changed."

He turned to walk out of the throne room and Misha started to walk after him, but Tizzy gripped her arm to stop her. "He's ok Misha," he said, "he just needs some time to cool down." As Leo walked away, Tom turned to Lord Pizzazz. "I think I have an idea," he said, "but it's going to be dangerous and we have to time it perfectly."

Lord Pizzazz started to chuckle, "Danger is my middle name," he said. Patience raised her eyebrows. "Yes, and look where danger has got you," she said pointing to his wheelchair. He looked down at his legs. "Yes, I suppose you're right," he said.

Back outside in the cave, Leo followed the same path that he had taken with Peppy earlier. He couldn't tell how late it was because the gems kept shining all night, but he was feeling tired. He noticed a treehouse in the branches of a tall yellow tree which seemed to be empty, so he decided to investigate. He passed a small apple tree and picked two of the apples from a branch and continued walking towards the treehouse.

There were steps leading up to the front door, so he made his way to the top and looked inside. There was one large room which was clean and tidy, and there were two small windows and a bed with some wooden furniture. It looked as though no one lived there, so he walked in and closed the curtains, then he placed the apples on a cupboard next to the bed. He rubbed his eyes and yawned then he got undressed and climbed in. The bed felt soft and warm, and apart from the sound of the birds singing in the distance, the treehouse was quiet, so he quickly fell asleep.

6 THE BADDEST BAD GUY EVER

Early the next morning Leo woke to the sound of a bird chirping outside of the window, so he stretched out his arms and legs and threw off the covers. He climbed out of the bed and he noticed his apples on the bedside table, so he grabbed one and took a bite, then he quickly dressed himself and walked over to the window. He slowly opened the curtains and just outside the window was a beautiful blue and yellow parrot.

"Oh, you're so cute," he said, "are you hungry?" The bird hopped onto the windowsill so Leo bit off a tiny piece of the apple and passed it through. The bird paused to look at him for a moment with its head to one side, then it quickly grabbed the piece of apple in its beak and flew up into the cave. Leo gazed across the cave and then he noticed the entrance to the echo tunnels that he had passed the day before.

He quickly put his shoes on and made his way out of the treehouse. He ran along the path as fast as his legs could carry him, and when he reached the entrance to the tunnels he stopped to look inside.

The walls were covered with jewels which cast light all around, so he took a few steps inside and then stared closely at one of the blue gemstones. He gently touched the stone to feel the smooth edges and he tapped it with his knuckles.

To his delight the stone rang out with a high-pitched humming sound which echoed through the tunnels. He saw a stick on the floor, so he picked it up and used it to tap another stone.

This had a different sound, so he tapped several more stones and each of them had their own sound. Leo laughed out loud.

"This is awesome," he said. His voice and his laughter echoed all around him which made him laugh even more. Soon the echo tunnels were filled with the sound of music and laughter as he ran up and town tapping every stone he could see.

On the other side of Viva City, Peppy was standing outside the entrance of the tunnel to grans house. Lord Pizzazz had sent her ahead of the group to begin the first phase of the mission while the others were getting ready.

She felt nervous as she turned to look around at the city behind her, but she reached into her pocket and took out the orange stone that she had found the day before.

She smiled to herself and remembered the journey she had taken with her friends, and as she turned to face the tunnel again, she had a more determined look on her face. "I hope this works," she said to herself. She took a deep breath and stepped alone into the tunnel and as she did, her hair began to glow lighting the way ahead.

Back at the temple, the others had gathered in the throne room wearing their cloaks. Lord Pizzazz was sat in his wheelchair wearing his golden cape, and Patience was holding onto some colored shirts. "You're all part of the rebellion now," she said as she passed them around, "you don't need the cloaks anymore, the shirts have a puzzle logo sewn into the sleeves and you should wear them with pride."

They all removed their cloaks and put on the shirts, and then Lord Pizzazz turned to look at Tom. "Are we all ready?" he asked. "We're still waiting for the doctor," he replied.

Suddenly the door to the throne room opened, and Leo ran into the room full of color and energy. "Hey guys," he called as he ran towards them, "you have to come and see the echo tunnels, they're amazing." Tom stepped forward. "We've got more important things to do today," he said, "maybe we could look later." Leo grabbed Misha by the hand. "It won't take long," he said, I made some really cool music and the tunnels were laughing, you're gonna love it."

Lord Pizzazz rolled across to him in his wheelchair. "You need to come with us," he said, "Tom can tell you the plan on the way to meet Peppy." Leo looked confused. "Where has she gone?" he asked. "She went to the Headquarters to create a distraction," he replied, "she's going to meet us there."

Leo was totally shocked. "Are you crazy?" he said. "Peppy knows what she's doing," explained Patience, "she's done this before." Leo turned and ran toward the door. "We need to stop her before it's too late, he shouted." "Wait," called Tom, "we have a plan." Leo didn't reply, he just kept running.

Lord Pizzazz Interrupted. "Let him go, we have to stick to the plan. When we get to the Headquarters I will hold back with Patience, then I'll give the signal when I'm ready." Leo ran out of the temple and along the path until he reached the entrance to the Tunnel.

He looked back into the cave wondering if he should wait for the others, then he shook his head and looked back into the tunnel.

Just at that moment, he saw a light and the Doctor emerged into the cave looking surprised to see Leo. "Where have you been?" asked Leo. "Well erm, I needed to erm, speak to gran about the plan," he said, "where are you going?" he continued trying to change the subject. "I need to rescue Peppy," he said, "she's in terrible danger." The Doctor passed his torch to Leo. "Well you had better take this with you," he said, and then he stepped to one side.

Leo looked up at the Doctor suspiciously for a moment, then he quickly grabbed the torch from him and ran into the tunnel. The light from the torch revealed flashes of the ancient paintings on the walls, and he could hear the crunching of his feet on the ground as he ran. He was less nervous about the tunnel this time and all he could think about was Peppy.

Eventually he reached the end of the tunnel and stood in front of the fireplace door. He thumped his hand on the back of the fireplace and waited for a moment, but there was no sound from the other side. He thumped again much harder this time and called out. "Gran are you even in there?" He paused to listen and there was a faint shuffling sound, then he could hear gran speaking as she approached. "All right, all right, these old legs don't move as quickly as they used to you know." There was a soft click from inside the cottage and the fireplace slid to one side.

Leo stepped inside and passed the torch to gran. "Thanks," he said, and then he ran across the room to open the front door.

Gran placed the torch by the fireplace and called after him. "Are you on your own?" she asked, as she pulled the rope to close the tunnel entrance.

"Yes, I've got to find Peppy," he said. "Don't you think it would be better to work as a team?" she asked. Leo shook his head.

"The others will get here soon, but I need to stop her before she gets into trouble." He turned to walk through the door, but Gran stopped him. "Before you go you should take something to eat," she said.

There was a large pile of sandwiches on a tray wrapped in foil, so she picked one of them up and passed it to him. He took the sandwich and put it in his pocket. "Thanks," he said.

"Peppy only left a few minutes ago," said gran, "but you won't catch her, she's probably halfway to the city by now." Leo looked puzzled, but he turned and ran into the forest. "Good luck," she called, and she closed the door behind him.

At Hum Drum City, Peppy had already arrived outside the Headquarters and was hiding behind some trees. She looked across to the side of the building, and there were two guards standing beside the hidden doorway.

She needed to create a distraction, so she reached into a small bag and took out some different colored spray paints. She looked at them with a cheeky smile, and then looked across to the front of the headquarters.

Her long blue hair started to glow and in an instant, there was a flash of blue as she ran across to the building. She quickly sprayed her slogans all over the walls, and the windows and doors. Some of the letters were as tall as her and she even managed to spray all over one of the guard's black cars.

It was all over in a matter of seconds, so Peppy needed to retreat to the trees and wait for the others.

However, Peppy was totally unaware that one of the Guards was waiting for her, holding onto a net gun. As she sped back to the trees, he fired the giant net and it instantly became entangled around her. She tripped over it and rolled across the ground coming to a stop at the trunk of a tree, and then she was immediately surrounded by a dozen of the General's guards.

The guard with the net gun stepped forward and looked down at her as she tried to free herself. "We've been expecting you," he said with a grin, then he turned to the others, "take her to the jail," he ordered, "the General will be pleased."

Meanwhile, Leo had just emerged from the forest and he stood on the road looking ahead to Hum Drum City. He was quite out of breath from all the running, but the City didn't look too far away. He reached into his pocket and took out the sandwich that gran had given to him. He took a bite as he walked along, then he kicked a stone across the road. It bounced into some grass and he remembered the colorful stones that Peppy had found.

He thought of the journey that he had taken with Peppy and the others and felt guilty that he had left his friends behind.

He looked up again towards the City, and with a determined look, he started walking a little faster.

Back at the Headquarters, Peppy was now stood in the jail. There wasn't much light and it felt cold and damp. She held onto the bars looking across at two of the guards in the hallway. They were searching through her belongings and talking to each other, and then Peppy heard a voice behind her in the jail. "How on earth did they catch you?"

Peppy turned to see a lady with long white hair and immediately recognized her. "Grace," she said, and she walked over to her, "the guards seemed to know I was coming, I was supposed to create a distraction, but now all of my friends are in danger and I can't warn them." One of the guards called out from the hallway. "No talking." Grace sat on the floor and spoke quietly.

"I think the General has a spy," she said, "it's the only way they could have known your plans." Peppy sat next to her and held her hand. "Don't worry," she said, "Lord Pizzazz is very clever, he'll know what to do.

They sat in silence for a few moments and then they heard some footsteps along the hallway. They looked up as General Median approached the jail, then he looked straight at Peppy with a menacing smile. "So, you are the one that's been causing all this trouble," he said, it's good to finally have you in my jail."

He turned to his guards. "What do you have for me?" he asked.

One of the guards passed Peppy's bag over to him. "Just these spray paints and some stones," he replied. General Median held the colored stones in his hand and gazed at them for a moment.

Peppy quickly stood up. "Those are mine," she said. The General laughed and wrapped the stones in a handkerchief. "You won't need these anymore," he said, "I think I'll keep them as a souvenir." He put them into his pocket. "Your days of spraying slogans are over, and soon you'll be melted down just like the others, you'll have no need for these silly colored stones."

Grace stood up next to Peppy. "Why are you so afraid of us?" she asked. "I'm not afraid of anything," he snapped, "but you should be afraid, I'll come back for you later, but first I need to meet with your husband, he's going to tell me the location of Viva City, and then we can put an end to your rebellion once and for all." Peppy stepped towards him. "You can't do this," she said. "I can and I will," he replied, "the doctor thinks he can save you all if he tells me where you live, but he's a fool." Peppy grabbed the bars of the jail. "You'll never get away with this," she said. General Median laughed to himself and then he walked away leaving them alone in the cold dark jail.

Back at the entrance to the forest, Lord Pizzazz and the others had started to make their way along the road to the City. Bruce was pushing Lord Pizzazz along in his wheelchair and Tom walked along beside them. Tom looked back at the others. "Remember the plan," he said, Peppy should have sprayed the building by now, so the hidden doorway will be unguarded. She'll meet us outside and we can sneak in while the guards are scrubbing the walls."

Lord Pizzazz agreed. "He's right," he said, Peppy has never let us down before, but I hope that she found Leo, if he tries to stop her the whole plan could fail." Misha looked at Tizzy with her fingers crossed. "I know," he said to her, "I hope he's ok too."

Leo had just arrived at the City and there were tall buildings all around him, and bustling streets with cars speeding in every direction. He had never been to the City before and there were people everywhere, walking in and out of buildings or standing in crowds. He felt quite overwhelmed by all the commotion, so he closed his eyes for a moment.

He could hear the cars hooting at each other, and the sound of a siren in the distance. Someone was speaking through a loudspeaker at the train station and people were chatting all around him. He could feel a cold breeze on the back of his neck and his feet were aching from the long walk. The smell from a hotdog stand wafted across and Leo opened his eyes. "It smells like sweaty armpits," he said to himself. Then he remembered why he was in the City, so he started walking.

He passed a man standing at a bus stop and decided to ask him for directions. "Excuse me, he said, "can you tell me how to get to the headquarters?" The man turned and looked down at Leo wearing his brightly colored clothes, then frowned and turned away without answering him. Leo didn't quite understand, but he continued along the pavement and then he saw a woman walking towards him pushing a pram. "Excuse me," he said. But before he could ask her, she quickened her pace and rushed past him.

"Weeesh," what's wrong with people," he said, "I suppose I'll just have to find it myself." He stepped forward to cross the road when suddenly a car horn screeched at him. He jumped back onto the pavement and fell onto the floor with a bump. The driver of the car waved his fist at Leo. "Why don't you look where you're going," he shouted. Then he sped off in a hurry.

Leo sat on the floor for a moment to calm himself, then he stood and brushed himself down. He continued along the pavement and then he noticed a very long black car parked at the side of the road. It was the longest car he had ever seen. It had at least ten blacked out windows along the side which looked like mirrors, and Leo could see his reflection looking back at him.

He walked towards the back of the car and looked in the glass for a moment, and then he smiled and started pulling faces at himself. He stood in various poses, and then he turned and looked over his shoulder while waving his butt in the air. At the same time, he started to sing a little tune. "Look at my butt, look at my butt, look at my butt, butt, butt."

Just then, the window lowered and a man with Grey hair and dark eyes looked across at him. Leo didn't realize that it was the General, but he was very embarrassed, so he quickly stopped what he was doing.

"That was an interesting little dance," said the General. Leo's face lit up. "I just invented it," he said, "I could do it again if you like." The general shook his head.

"That won't be necessary," he said, and then he smiled at him, "what's your name?" he asked. "You're a stranger," replied Leo, "I shouldn't tell you my name." The general paused and then he smiled again. "What are you doing out here on your own?" he asked. "I'm looking for my friend Peppy, "I think she's at the Headquarters."

The general paused for a moment and then he leaned out of the window looking from side to side with shifty eyes.

"My name is Tom Median and I work at the Headquarters. I can assure you that there's no one there called Peppy. Now that I'm not a stranger anymore," he continued, "you can tell me your name." Then he gave Leo a friendly smile.

"My name is Leo," he replied." The General looked pleasantly surprised when he heard his name. "Are you sure you haven't seen her? she's got long blue hair." He continued as he stepped closer to the car. "I'm afraid I have not," the general replied, "but I have been looking for you, the people at Bootcamp have been very worried since you ran away with your friends."

He opened the car door and tapped on the seat with his hand. "Why don't you jump in and I can take you to the Headquarters. Once we get there, I'll call your parents and they can come and get you." Leo frowned at him. "I have to find Peppy first," he said. "Well I can help you with that," replied the General," If you tell me where she lives, I can take her home."

Leo paused for a moment to think. "Peppy told me that you hate us, and that you put people in jail and melt them down."

The General looked shocked. "That's not true," he said, "I would never do that, I'm the prime master of the world, I think your friends are making up stories, why don't you come with me and I'll prove it to you." Leo was still suspicious, but he nodded and climbed into the car.

The inside of the car was huge and there was a television screen at one end. There was a telephone next to a drink's cabinet, and just above this, there was a glass panel which separated them from the driver. The General called out to him. "Take us to the headquarters." The driver looked into his mirror and nodded, and then he pulled away.

Leo looked at the General and decided to tell him about his castle. "When we find Peppy I'm going to take her home and marry her," he said, I'll build a castle right in the middle of Viva City, and she'll be my queen and everyone can have parties every night,"....

Leo continued talking and the General pretended to listen. He picked up his phone and he spoke quietly to the guard at the other end. "I have a change of plan," he said, "take the girl to the top floor and wait for my return." Then he pressed some other buttons on the phone and spoke to someone else in a clearer voice.

"I have found one of our runaways," he said, "could you let Leo's parents know that we have found him, and that they need to make their way to the Headquarters." He put the phone down and he looked at Leo. "It won't be much longer Leo," he said, "I promise you'll be reunited with your friends soon."

Back at the Headquarters, Peppy and Grace were still sat on the jail floor. Two of the guards approached to unlock the door, and then they rushed in to grab Peppy.

She struggled but they were too strong, so Grace tried to grab her and pull her back. One of the guards pushed Grace to the ground and looked at Peppy. "You've got too much energy," he said, "we'll soon take that away from you."

They dragged her away locking the door to the Jail behind them, and led her to a staircase, they climbed the stairs and walked into a hallway which had several office doors either side. Peppy could see that there were a few people sitting at their desks typing or speaking on the phone, but the guards continued towards the lobby at the front of the building. Once they reached the lobby, they stopped outside an elevator and one of the guards pushed the button to the top floor. The doors opened and they stepped inside with Peppy.

Just as the door had closed, the General's car pulled up outside the Headquarters. Leo stepped out closely followed by the General and he looked up at the building with his mouth wide open. "Oh, my O.M.G," he said. It seemed to be wider at the top than it was at the bottom, and he could see the symbol with the black 'X' rotating slowly on the roof.

General Median looked down at him. "Come inside and I'll take you to the canteen for something to eat while you wait for your parents," he said. There were a couple of steps leading into the building and as they walked through the doors to the lobby, Leo could see one or two people busy shuffling around holding clipboards. There was a large rug on the floor with a reception desk to one side, and there were several glass doors leading to other rooms. At the end of the lobby there was a wide staircase and an elevator which was next to the doors to the canteen.

They crossed the lobby to the canteen and the General held the door open for Leo. As he stepped in, the General called over to one of the cooks.

"Bring this boy anything he wants to eat, I need to make a phone call and I'll be back soon," he said. The cook nodded anxiously. "Yes sir, right away sir," she replied. He looked back at Leo. "Don't go anywhere, I'll be back soon." Then he closed the door and walked away.

Leo looked up to the cook. "Can I really have anything I want?" he asked. "Of course you can," she replied. Leo became very excited and sat at one of the tables. "This is the best day ever," he shouted.

Meanwhile, outside the Headquarters Lord Pizzazz and the others had just arrived and were standing behind some trees.

"Where are the guards?" asked Tom, "and where are the slogans on the walls?" Lord Pizzazz wheeled his chair forward to take a closer look. "It's too quiet," he said, "I'll make my way to the front of the building with Patience while you all get to the hidden doorway." Tizzy suddenly became very anxious and started shaking and sniffing with fear. "Be careful," he said. Patience pushed Lord Pizzazz through the trees while the others made their way to the side of the building.

They approached the hidden doorway and Bruce grabbed the handle, but the door was locked. Suddenly, he was hit in the chest with two tiny spikes which were attached to some wires, and he immediately collapsed to the floor unable to move. At the other end of the wires was a guard holding onto an electrical Taser Gun. "It's a trap", shouted Tizzy, "we have to go back."

Misha immediately disappeared, then Tom, Tizzy and the doctor started to run. They only managed a few steps and were surrounded by the guards. Tizzy was more anxious than he had ever been before, he was constantly twitching and sniffing, and his hair began to glow bright green. Some of the guards were pointing their electrical Taser Guns at them and then one of them spoke.

"What are you going to do now?" he asked, and then he started to laugh at them. He stepped a little closer to Tizzy. "Are you scared," he said, "you should be, we're going to melt you down with all of your friends." All of the guards started laughing at them and then Tizzy clenched his fists with an overwhelming sense of anger. "Just let us go," he shouted. "Oh, I don't think so," the guard replied, "I think we'll start by cutting off that silly hair of yours."

Tizzy's hair grew even brighter and his eyes turned a shade of green. His fear and his anger became too much for him, so he threw out his hands and shouted. "Let us go," As he did a powerful rush of air left his body, lifting the guards from the ground and throwing them at least 20 feet into the air.

Tom and the doctor couldn't quite believe what they were seeing as the guards were scattered around the outside of the building. "That's it," said Tizzy, "I've had enough," and he ran towards the guards in a frenzy of emotion, knocking them down like skittles.

The last of the guards was standing over Bruce, pinning him to the ground with his Taser Gun. Tizzy held out his hands and used all his power to lift the guard and throw him towards the trees.

There was a moment of silence, then Tom and the doctor approached Tizzy. "Where on earth did that come from," said Tom excitedly. "I don't like bullies," he replied. Bruce picked himself up off the floor. "Let's get this door open," he said.

He gripped the handle and pulled the whole door out of the wall and dropped it on to the floor.

As they all stepped inside the hidden doorway, they were confronted by several more guards. Tizzy tried to use his powers, but he was too late.

They were all hit with nets and Tasers and the guards quickly overpowered them. Soon their arms were chained behind their backs and they were thrown into the jail.

7 KING OF THE WORLD

Back at the lobby, General Median had just heard about the capture of Leo's friends, so he made his way back to the canteen. He opened the glass doors and as he looked across at Leo, he could see that the cook was stood beside him and his table was completely covered in food. The cook suddenly noticed the General and looked up at him. "He ordered almost everything on the menu," she said nervously.

The General walked towards them. "What's that?" he asked, as he looked down at the arrangement of food on the table. Leo looked up. "It's a map of Viva City," he said, "It looks exactly the same." The General smiled to himself. "That's good to know," he replied, and then he looked at the cook. "Go and fetch a camera, this is so good I think we should take a picture." He put his hand on Leo's shoulder. "Let's make our way upstairs," he said," we can wait there for your parents." Leo stood up and they made their way out of the canteen.

As they walked across the lobby to the elevator, Leo tripped and fell over creating a cloud of dust. He looked down at his feet and he noticed a small bulge in the rug. "I knew that would happen," he said, and then he sneezed. "Yes," replied the General, "but the best way to clean up the mess is to sweep it under the rug." Leo picked himself up and then he sneezed again, so the General reached into his pocket. "Here, he said, "have a tissue."

As he pulled out his handkerchief, Peppy's orange stone fell out and rolled on to the floor in front of Leo. He picked it up and immediately recognized it, so he looked up at the General. "This is Peppy's stone," he said. "I don't know what you're talking about," replied the General, "let's just go upstairs." Leo took a step back. "You've been lying to me the whole time," he said, "where's Peppy?" The General reached forward and tried to grab him. "Just come with me," he snapped. Leo turned and he quickly ran out of the lobby into one of the hallways.

General Median calmly walked over to a telephone and picked it up. He was about to speak to his guards, but then he was interrupted by a voice calling from the front of the building. "You wanted to see me General, here I am." He looked across to the front doors of the lobby to see Lord Pizzazz sitting outside in his wheelchair with the love of his life standing beside him. One of the guards answered the phone. "What do you need General?" he asked. "Send all of your guards to the front of the building," he replied, "we finally have Lord Pizzazz." He put the phone down and walked over to greet them.

"My beautiful Patience," he said as he stepped outside, you've finally returned to me." Just as he spoke, his guards appeared from both sides of the building and surrounded them. "We're just here to talk," replied Patience, then she grabbed the wheelchair and pushed it towards him.

As she approached the door's she realized that there were some steps, so she stopped and looked up at the General. He chuckled to himself and then he clicked his fingers at one of the guards. "Go and fetch a ramp or something," he said, and he looked down at Lord Pizzazz with a cruel grin.

While the guards were helping the General, Leo had managed to run through the building unnoticed. He found the door to the basement, and he ran down the stairway that led to the jail. He stopped at the bottom and then he slowly crept forward. As he looked into the jail, he could see his friends with their arms chained behind their backs.

"Leo," said Tizzy, "I'm so glad you're ok." Leo looked around the Jail. "Where's Peppy?" he asked. Grace stepped forward. "The guards have taken her to the top floor to be melted down, I don't know how much time we have left," she said.

Leo noticed that Bruce was trying to free himself from the chains; they were the biggest chains that Leo had ever seen. "I need your help to rescue Peppy," said Bruce. "But how am I supposed to get you all out?" replied Leo.

Just at that moment he heard the sound of keys behind him and he turned around, but no one was there. Suddenly Misha appeared in front of him smiling and holding the jail keys. "Misha," said Leo excitedly, "you did it again, you are so awesome." She held up a picture of a love heart, so he threw his arms around her.

Bruce called out to them. "I hate to break up your reunion," he said impatiently, "but are you going to let us out?" Leo let Misha go and she stepped over to the jail to open the door, then she used the keys to free her friends one by one. Tom rubbed his sore wrists and looked over to Leo. "You need to get to the top floor," he said, "Bruce and Misha can go with you, while Grace and the Doctor head for Viva City, and I'll go with Tizzy to distract the guards." Bruce and Misha both nodded in agreement.

"Are you sure you're going to be alright?" asked Leo. Tom looked across at Tizzy and smiled. "We'll be fine," he said, "we have our secret weapon." Leo looked a little confused, but he shrugged his shoulders and looked over to Bruce and Misha. "Let's go" he said. Tom and Tizzy ran outside with Grace and the Doctor while the others ran back towards the stairs.

At the lobby, Patience had just managed to get Lord Pizzazz inside and was pushing his wheelchair. General Median walked alongside them and three of his guards followed them in. Lord Pizzazz looked up at the General. "We need to reach a truce between your people and mine," he said, "you can't keep melting people down, we're not all supposed to be the same." The General stopped. "I disagree," he replied, "an efficient and productive world can only be built with order and discipline, if everyone is the same then there would be no more wars and no more rebellions."

Patience turned to him. "If everyone was the same, there would be no imagination or creativity, and no desire to change things for the better." Lord Pizzazz agreed. "We just want everyone to accept each other, and to be ourselves without fear or isolation."

The General looked over to his guards and nodded. They quickly stepped forward and grabbed Patience and the wheelchair, and then General Median knelt down in front of Lord Pizzazz. "You're a fool if you think I'll ever stop, soon you'll see things differently." He looked up at his guards. "Take them upstairs," he ordered.

Just then, he heard a noise behind him and turned to look. Bruce and Leo appeared on the other side of the lobby. He had completely forgotten about Leo and was totally shocked. "Stop them," he shouted to his guards. They immediately let go of Patience and the wheelchair and ran towards them with their Taser Guns.

Bruce knew what was coming, so he reached over to a door and pulled it out of the wall, then he held it in front of himself and Leo. The tiny spikes from the Taser Guns struck the door, and then Bruce swung it around knocking the guards off their feet. They both ran across the lobby to the stairs with Bruce still holding on to the door. Leo looked at the buttons to the elevator. "It's on the top floor," he said, "we'll have to use the stairs."

As they ran up the stairs, General Median decided to run after them himself, but he was tripped over by Patience and he fell to the floor. He looked back at her angrily, and then he glanced across to the main doors. Tizzy was outside throwing the guards around like ragdolls, and Tom was beside him. The General thumped his fist on the floor out of frustration, and then he picked himself up and pushed Patience to the floor. "This isn't over," he said, and he ran towards the stairs.

Bruce and Leo had reached the top floor of the Headquarters and as they ran through the General's office, two more guards emerged from a small door at the other end of the room. "That must be where Peppy is," said Leo. Bruce threw the door towards the guards and knocked them down. They ran across to the door and Bruce knocked it down with one kick.

Peppy was in front of them strapped to the chair and ready for meltdown. "Bruce, Leo," she called, "we have to shut it down, the control panel is in the corner." They both looked across the room. "I'll get Peppy out of the chair," said Bruce. Leo nodded and ran over to the control panel. "There's too many buttons," he said, "which one to I push?" Peppy looked over to him as Bruce ripped the wires from the chair. "I don't know," she replied, "but we're running out of time, just hit something."

Leo gazed over the control panel and he noticed a big red button in the center. "Emergency only," he said to himself. He looked over at Bruce and Peppy, and then he looked back at the red button. He raised his hand and then suddenly General Median appeared at the door.

"Stop!" he shouted, "if you hit that button, you'll destroy the whole building and kill us all." Peppy stood up from the chair. "All you ever do is tell lies," she said, "we'll never follow your rules, it's over."

General Median started to slowly creep into the room. "I am the Prime Master, and if you think you'll get away with this, you've got another thing coming."

Just then, a red fire extinguisher hit him on the back of the head, knocking him to the floor, and then Misha appeared behind him. Bruce smiled at her. "I thought he would never shut up," he said. "come on Leo, let's finish this."

Leo looked at the red button and took a deep breath, and then he struck it with his hand as hard as he could.

They waited for a few seconds and the device started shaking violently, then it grew brighter and a deep humming sound filled the room. They all covered their ears and then the device exploded sending a whirlwind of color and energy into the air crashing through the roof. It sent rubble flying into the air and then it started to fall back towards the building.

Leo looked at Peppy and Bruce, then he ran as fast as he could and leaped towards the chair, just as the rubble came crashing down on top of them.

The rays of color soared into the sky breaking up the clouds and releasing the sunshine on to the City below.

Meanwhile, Leo's parents were just arriving at the City, and they could see beams of color sweeping across the sky in every direction. "What on earth is that?" asked Leo's father. "I have no idea," she replied, "but it looks like it's coming from the direction of Headquarters."

Some of the rays of color dropped out of the sky hitting people and restoring the color that was once taken from them. Hope was standing beside gran outside her cottage at the foot of the mountain and looking across to the City. A beam of color passed right through her and her orange hair returned, and at the same time the colors found their way into the lobby and passed through Patience.

Eventually, the rainbows of color had disappeared over the horizon and all around the City there were hundreds of people with their color restored.

On the top floor of Headquarters in the meltdown room, the dust had settled, and all was quiet. Leo, Peppy and Bruce were safe and huddled together under the protection of Leo's bubble. Leo stood up and his bubble disappeared, then they all looked at the destruction in the room. The sun was casting a light through the roof and the Auto Suppression Device was smashed. "We did it," said Peppy excitedly.

"Yeah, that wasn't so hard," said Leo, and then he reached into his pocket and pulled out her orange stone. "I think this is yours," he said.

They all heard a noise from just inside the other room and turned to look. General Median was lying motionless on the floor covered in dust, but just beyond him they could see Misha moving and rubbing her head.

Leo quickly ran past the general and helped her to sit up, then he sat next to her and held her hands. "You will always be my best friend Misha, I love you," he said. She looked back at him and smiled. "I'll always love you too Leo," she replied.

Leo looked at her in total shock with his mouth open, but then he just smiled and said nothing. "Group Hug," shouted Peppy and she ran over to them. Bruce followed and they all huddled together on the floor. "Not so tight Bruce," said Leo.

Down in the lobby, Patience and Lord Pizzazz were waiting for them to return, and Tom and Tizzy were just joining them. "Did you take care of all the guards?" asked Patience. "Yes," said Tizzy, they won't be bothering us for a while. Patience looked up as Leo's parents came running into the lobby. "What are you two doing here?" asked Tom. "We had a call from someone to say that Leo was here," replied his mother "is he alright?"

There was a sound from the other end of the room, and they all turned to see the elevator doors open, then Leo and the others stepped out into the lobby. "Mummy, daddy," shouted Leo and he ran over to greet them. "Where have you been?" asked his father. "Well, we ran away from Bootcamp because they were evil," he replied, "and then we met our new friends and walked all the way to Viva City, and then we had to stop the General from melting us all down, so Lord Pizzazz came up with a plan to stop him and free the ASD."

Lord Pizzazz wheeled his chair towards them. "Actually, it was all Tom's idea," he said, he realized that it had to be an inside job, so we needed to get caught, Misha was the most important part of the plan, her invisibility meant that she could get the jail keys and release Bruce. However, we had no idea about Tizzy's powers and didn't expect Leo to run off to rescue Peppy."

Leo's parents looked totally puzzled then Tom stepped forward. "Oh, well, it all worked out in the end," he said, "but what happened to the General?" "We left him on the floor upstairs," said Bruce, "and the device is completely destroyed."

Leo stood in front of everyone. "So, what are we going to do now?" he asked enthusiastically. "I think we need to go home," said his mother. Leo looked around at his friends, and then he had an idea. "We don't need to go back to Stormless," he replied, "we can live at Viva City." Leo's parents still looked confused and a little bit unsure. "What do you mean?" asked his father. Lord Pizzazz moved his wheelchair closer. "It's not a bad idea, Viva City is a magical place beneath Shadow Mountain where you can live, and work." Patience moved forward and stood next to Lord Pizzazz. "There would be no more grey skies and no more rules," she said, "and Leo would have everything that he needs."

His parents looked around at his friends and looked at each other, and then they smiled and nodded. "Awesome," shouted Leo and then he gave them a hug. "I'm telling my parents too," added Tizzy. "And me," said Tom. Misha just held up a card with a thumbs up.

Lord Pizzazz started to remove his golden cape from around his shoulders then he passed it to Leo.

I've done my part for Viva City," he said, "now it's time to pass on the responsibility to someone else and I can't think of anyone better than you." He leaned forward and put his hand on Leo's shoulder. "I name you king Leo," he said.

Leo took the cape and looked back at him. "Is this for real? He asked. Lord Pizzazz chuckled to himself. Peppy will be your adviser and Bruce will stay as head of security, me and Patience are going back to Viva City to find Hope, and then we'll travel the world." He looked up from his chair and smiled at Patience. "It's about time we had a break," he said.

Leo threw the cape over his shoulders and then Peppy and Misha walked forward to hold his hands. Peppy nudged him. "What's the first thing you're going to do as King of Viva City?" she asked, get married? Build a castle? Leo thought for a moment and then he smiled. "Come here," he said. He walked over to the front doors of the lobby and everyone else followed. They all looked out through the glass towards the City. "I'm going to climb to the top of Shadow Mountain," he said. Tom once again shook his head in disbelief. "Come on," he said, "let's go home."

A short distance away, a long black car was parked by the side of the road. In the back seat a battered and dusty looking General Median looked through the rear window across to the Headquarters and saw them all leaving through the front doors of the building. He turned and leant forward to tap on the glass to the driver. "It's time to go," he said." Then he turned back to look through the window. "Make no mistake Lord Pizzazz," he said to himself, "this isn't over." The driver slowly pulled away and General Median frowned as he watched them disappear into the distance.

THE END

VIVACITY

ABOUT THE AUTHOR

John Court lives in Kent with his wife and 3 children. He has spent most of his career working for the NHS in various professional roles and has a passion for equality and all things Autistic. He loves Movies, music and reading children's books to his Autistic son. Always known as 'a bit of a dreamer' as a child, John has used his imagination and his experiences with Autism to create a truly unique story. This book gives the reader a taste of the many struggles faced by Autistic children and their families in a light-hearted and fun way.

Printed in Great Britain
by Amazon

38083057R00054